GYPSY LOVER

When Rina Morrison was browbeaten by her family into marriage, she resigned herself to a loveless — though wealthy — existence in Hungary. And after a devastating encounter with the dashing Michael an even more heart-wrenching future lay ahead, betrothed to one man whilst loving another. But did Michael really love her? In reality he was Miska the Gypsy and his bitterest enemy was Rina's fiancé. It was possible that his love for her might very well be hatred . . .

DENISE ROBINS

GYPSY LOVER

Complete and Unabridged

LINFORD
Leicester

First published in the United States of America

First Linford Edition
published 2008

British Library CIP Data

Robins, Denise, *1897* –
    Gypsy lover.—Large print ed.—
    Linford romance library
    1. Triangles (Interpersonel relations)—Fiction
    2. Love stories
    3. Large type books
    I. Title
    823.9'12 [F]

    ISBN 978–1–84782–488–2

Published by
F. A. Thorpe (Publishing)
Anstey, Leicestershire

Set by Words & Graphics Ltd.
Anstey, Leicestershire
Printed and bound in Great Britain by
T. J. International Ltd., Padstow, Cornwall

This book is printed on acid-free paper

1

When Rina Morrison stood in the hall of the Hotel Sacher in Vienna reading the letter handed to her by the reception-clerk, and discovered that her *fiancé* was not there to meet her as he had promised, her first reaction was one of relief.

She realized that it was all wrong. Here she was, young, beautiful, romantic, a dreamer of the sweetest, wildest dreams. She ought to have come out to Vienna, *en route* for Budapest, thrilled and exhilarated by the knowledge that a good-looking husband, a castle in Hungary, and unlimited wealth awaited her.

But she could not work up the vestige of a thrill. She felt definitely relieved that Lionel was not there, that she would not have to spend the rest of the journey with him.

She read the last half of his apologetic letter:

So sorry that you should have to travel to the Castle alone, darling, but as my mother is seriously ill, I cannot leave her. Take the Rapide straight through to Budapest. My chauffeur will meet you and drive you up to the mountains. I long for our meeting . . .

Rina tore up the letter and looked towards the crowded lounge. There was no doubt in her mind that Lionel Quest longed for their meeting. He had told her that he counted the hours until she would be with him. And she knew that he loved her — as surely as she realized that she could never love him.

'It isn't fair,' she told herself. 'I wanted life, a lover, love that would obliterate everything else — and I'm marrying for money.'

Rina did not want wealth. She had always longed for the luxuries and comforts of life which had been denied her — but her dreams had meant more to her than money. If it had not been for her family, she would not have crossed her own village square — let alone Europe — to marry Lionel Quest.

The family had put up a strong argument. Her mother persuaded her that it was a 'marvellous match'. Her father, floundering in a sea of financial depression, openly admitted that it would be a godsend. He was heavily in debt.

It was less than three months ago that Rina had met Lionel. He had been motoring through Aversham when his car broke down near the Morrisons' house. Lionel, hot and angry at the delay, had seen Rina in the garden with the sun on her red curls, her white tennis shorts accentuating her slender figure, and had been agreeably surprised to find such beauty in the remote English village. Five minutes later they were walking together to the nearest garage, and Lionel knew that he had met the only girl whom he had ever wanted to marry.

Rina admitted that she was impressed by his aristocratic good looks, his big white Mercédès, and his obvious adoration of her. But she did not fall in love with him.

He told her of his castle in the Hungarian mountains, where he and his family had lived for generations. She thrilled to his descriptions of the country, of the great treeless plains ringed by mountains where huge droves of cattle and horses grazed, guarded by mounted herdsmen or *Csikos*. But when, only a few weeks later, he asked her to marry him, she said, 'No.' She did not love him. She wanted him to realize that she could not make him happy.

It was a crushing blow to the family. They liked and respected Lionel Quest, and had watched his pursuit of Rina with almost hysterical anticipation. It seemed fantastic to them that any girl could turn him — and what he had to offer — down.

Lionel returned to Hungary without Rina, but refused to give up hope. A string of letters and telegrams followed her. Every night the Aversham exchange was booked for a long call from Hungary.

It was more than the family could stand. The atmosphere in the little house was tense and electric. Mrs. Morrison stormed and pleaded in turn.

Was there not a young sister still at school? A brother without a job?

Rina's father, faced with bankruptcy, prevailed upon her to change her mind. He argued that it was her duty to look after their interests as well as her own.

At last their arguments wore Rina down. She gave in, almost believing that her father was right. It probably was her duty, she decided, to marry Lionel Quest.

But now as she stood alone in the hotel at Vienna, on her way to meet him, she wondered if she had not been a weak fool. The prospect of the life she must lead in future terrified her. She knew she could never care in the way he would want or expect her to. It was a bitter pill which Fate, backed up by the family, was forcing her to swallow. A pill which would be offered her on a golden spoon bearing the Quest coat of arms. But now it was too late. She must make the rest of the journey to Hungary and resign herself to the future.

Turning to the bureau, she asked the clerk about her reservation on the Budapest *Rapide*. The man excused himself with a smile.

'If Madame will wait one moment. I am just attending to this gentleman's requirements.'

Rina glanced at the man who stood next to her at the desk. He was an amazingly handsome creature — tall, with thick black hair brushed back from a tanned forehead. He spoke fluent German to the clerk, but she was sure he was neither German nor Viennese. He looked Latin.

'I beg your pardon,' she said. 'I didn't notice that you were making enquiries.'

The stranger looked down at her and

smiled. He said in perfect English:

'It's my fault for being so long. I've been bombarding this unfortunate fellow with questions, but I am finished now. Forgive me for having kept you waiting.'

Rina watched him walk through the lounge before she turned to the clerk.

'What a very interesting-looking man,' she said. 'Do you know who he is?'

The clerk shook his head.

'I don't know, Madame, except that he is from Hungary.'

'From Hungary?' she said curiously.

'Yes, Madame. He goes back tonight by barge.'

'But how thrilling! Can one go by barge to Budapest?'

'Certainly, Madame,' the clerk told her. 'It takes much longer of course. Two or three days.'

'It must be heaven,' she said enthusiastically. 'The Blue Danube! I long to see it.'

The clerk nodded.

'It is said to be the loveliest river in the world.'

Rina half closed her eyes. She envied the handsome stranger his trip on the barge. But then it was impossible to imagine him travelling to Budapest in an overcrowded, conventional train. He was so obviously a man who had woven the correct design for living. She would gamble on that. And she would gamble that the key to the design spelt 'freedom'.

Freedom! Rina smiled bitterly. That was what she had always sought for — in vain. In Aversham she had rebelled against the narrow, hemmed-in life of the village. She had grown to loathe the complacent, smug attitude of her friends. The constant round of tennis and bridge parties where one saw the same old faces bored her. During the last few years she had managed to drift away from them, and had gained the reputation for being a recluse. That did not worry her. She was happier in her own room, or in a secluded corner

8

of the garden where she could dream her dreams and build her 'castles in the air'.

They had been wonderful castles, very like the one which Lionel had described to her. But always in the dream castles she was married to the man she loved. That castle had been merely a background to her lover.

Now her hours of freedom were rushing past. If she went by train she would be with Lionel tomorrow morning. But if she went by barge it would mean another three days of liberty. And it would be so lovely to go down the Danube — to see life — *real* life — perhaps real romance.

Rina made up her mind at that moment. She would go by barge. She would snatch at her last chance of liberty.

There was no definite desire at the back of her mind just then to follow the attractive stranger. She might never see him on board. It was something deeper, fundamentally, that made her cancel her reservation on the *Rapide* and book a cabin on that barge. The thrill of freedom, of adventure, of all that would be denied her once she was the wife of Lionel Quest.

She wired to Lionel that she would be three days late. She would explain when she saw him — no explanations now. Then she collected her luggage and took a taxi to the quay.

It was with a queer feeling of excitement that she boarded one of the old grey barges which take passengers and cargo down the broad, shining river through Austria and Hungary. She felt it was a crazy thing to have done; but when they were moving quietly away from Vienna she stood on deck, looking about her with bright, eager eyes, and was glad — terribly glad — that she had come.

The night was perfect, warm and windless. The river, jewelled with moonlight, reflected the red and green glow of lights from other passing barges and boats. Opposite her lay the dark shadow of the shore . . . woodland . . . forest, hill and an occasional old castle with gardens sloping down to the water. Like a scene from a Hans Andersen fairy-tale, she thought. And no Lionel or his mother to worry her — nothing to jar her nerves.

Rina leaned over the rail and lit a cigarette. She felt that life was good. One could forget everything on a night like this. The gentle lapping of the water against the boat fascinated her. Then suddenly she turned and looked over her shoulder. A shadow had fallen between her and the moon.

'This is a surprise,' said a rich, musical voice. 'You too, are journeying by barge to Hungary?'

She recognized the tanned face of the man from the hotel. The colour rose to her cheeks.

'Yes.' She smiled. 'I'm going to Budapest.'

'That's grand,' he said. 'You're wise to have chosen the river. Think of a train on a night like this!'

Rina looked up at the stars.

'I was thinking that the Danube — this river-trip — is the most exciting thing that has ever happened to me,' she said softly.

The man looked at her critically. She was very lovely, this English girl. That small vivid face with the *retroussé* nose was fascinating. Her figure in well-cut tweeds was perfect. If ever he had pictured a woman he could love madly, it was a woman like this one — young and fresh, with red hair, green eyes, and skin like white satin.

'You are going to live in Hungary?' he asked.

'Yes,' she said.

'Then Hungary is fortunate.'

Their eyes met. Rina felt her heart quicken. What was the matter with her? She was being crazy. But she found herself eager to smile back at him.

'You live there, too?' she asked.

'Yes, in the far mountains. I love Hungary. It's a wild, splendid country — lawless, in many parts.'

'That sounds frightening!'

'Not so frightening as the word 'law' to me.'

'What do you mean?'

'That no sane person can want to be hidebound by convention.'

His words found an echo in her heart. She agreed with him. She was so dreading her life with Lionel and his essentially conventional family. But for the next three days she was determined to forget about the future. Nothing would be allowed to spoil her days and nights on the Danube. She was still free; she could do what she wanted until they reached Budapest.

Free to do what? To travel beside this attractive man who lived in the Hungarian mountains and led a lawless existence? To take what life and the fates offered?

'I agree with you,' she said. 'But it's difficult not to be conventional in this civilized world.'

'Of course it is. But thank heaven we can't be too civilized on this old barge.

The Danube just wouldn't stand for it!'

'I don't believe it would,' she laughed. 'But would it be too conventional if I asked you your name?'

'Michael,' he said. He offered no other.

'I am Rina . . . '

'Rina,' he repeated. 'That's a very sweet name.'

She had never thought of it as 'sweet'. But when he said it in his rich, haunting voice, she felt that it sounded both sweet and exciting.

Michael! Who was he? Why did he live in Hungary? Where did he come from? She did not know. She did not care. She only felt gloriously free tonight and glad to be alive. Lionel was forgotten.

A gong reverberated from below. Michael said:

'That's the evening meal. And very good food one gets for such a small craft. Do you like Hungarian cooking? *Goulash . . . paprika . . . ?*' He smiled.

'I don't think I've tried it.'

'Oh, then there's a treat in store for you. I shall introduce you to our national dishes. And what about Tokay?'

Rina smiled back at him.

'I think I drank that once when an uncle of mine took me to an Hungarian restaurant in London.'

'It's a warm sweet wine. Come and drink a toast with me.'

She went with him gladly. It was so much more exciting to have a companion like this instead of being alone on the barge. In any case there were few other passengers, and it might have been a dull journey for her beyond the pleasure of the glorious scenery.

There were only half a dozen tables in the small dining-saloon. One was occupied by a German family. Rina liked the look of them. A fat, jolly father with two fat jolly little girls who had long flaxen pigtails.

At another table there were some men whom, Michael told her, were journalists from Budapest. He knew them by sight. They had just been to

Nuremberg to hear Hitler's speech. The other passengers he did not know, but there was one young couple who sat nearby, and spoke Hungarian, and were obviously on their honeymoon. They looked across the table at each other with rapt gaze.

Michael pointed out this pair, a lazy, amused smile on his lips.

'There you have the way in which to go down the Danube . . . a man and a woman in love . . . they are sensible!'

Rina was silent, crumbling a roll with small nervous fingers. She was nervous . . . she knew not quite why . . . and very exhilarated! Every word that this man Michael said to her had a strange and intense reaction upon her. She felt that she was no longer the Rina who had left England to marry Lionel. She was a stranger, even to herself . . . a person intoxicated by life . . . by the sheer joy of living.

Yes, Michael was right. To be in love with somebody and go down the Danube together on this barge . . . that would be perfect!

Every time her gaze met the eyes of the man who sat opposite her, her heart seemed to turn over in her body. Was she not going down the Danube under the most ideal conditions? she asked herself.

The food was queer, exciting, and she liked it. Liked the spices and peculiar flavours. Michael poured Tokay into her goblet and proposed a toast:

'To you and to your visit to my beloved country.'

'Thank you,' she said breathlessly.

They touched glasses. He drained his to the dregs. But she only sipped hers, for she was unused to wine and was afraid that it would go to her head. Everything was going to her head tonight.

Michael proved himself an entertaining companion during that meal. He could talk on most subjects. He touched on politics. Everybody was talking about the unrest in Europe and he was bored by it, he said. Hungary was standing by Germany now. He was sorry for the Viennese. Afraid for all the Balkan States who might be dragged into a world war. Too much discussion was futile. What was to be — was to be! But if he was ever called upon to fight, he would fight.

'And it might be against my country,' Rina reminded him.

'Ah!' he said. 'That's why I don't want to talk about politics. It's not the right subject for a beautiful woman. I could never fight against *you*.'

She caught her lower lip between her teeth and laughed.

'I wonder! You have the look of a man who could fight anything and anybody.'

'And you have the look of a girl who could stand up to it. You're rather brave really, taking this trip alone. I shall drink another toast' — he poured out some more of the golden wine — 'to Beauty, who travels alone to a country where all true Beauty may be found.'

The meal went on, full of badinage from Michael; of low happy laughter from Rina, and a sense of companionship and understanding increasing between them in some mysterious fashion.

Rina would have nothing to worry about on this trip . . . she could see that. Michael took possession of her . . . let her want for nothing . . . and had all the stewards on board at his command. He spent money in an extravagant cavalier fashion. The servants rushed to do his bidding. They called him 'Excellency'. Rina could not make out whether it was because he actually owned that title or because he spent his money so lavishly that they conferred the honour upon him just for the journey! He saw to it that, after dinner, comfortable chairs were placed up on the deck for them. There, coffee and liqueurs were brought out so that they could sit and enjoy the moonlight on the river and the warm lovely night.

Hungarians adore music, and Rina found that even this little barge was not without its Tzigane band. They played the wild stirring melodies of their country late into the night. It all seemed to her like a heavenly dream. With every hour that went by, she grew more thankful that she had abandoned the train journey to Budapest in favour of this trip.

Michael was obviously a man of moods. For an hour after dinner he sat quietly beside her, smoking, talking. And how well he talked! What stories he had to tell! What songs he could sing ... here and there picking up the strains of some Hungarian folk-song which the band was playing. He made her think of a little verse which she had once heard:

And each time her courage
  seemed to fail
Or whenever things were wrong,
He always told a more wonderful
  tale
Or sang a more wonderful song.

Then his mood changed and he became restless, unable to sit quietly

20

and converse. He wanted to dance. The music was getting into his blood, he said. They were playing a Hungarian waltz.

'Dance with me,' he said to Rina.

He gave her no time to make any conventional reply . . . to say that it was so long since she had danced . . . or that she did not know the new steps. He just swung her into his arms and took her down the smooth deck, whirling her into the quick steps of an old-fashioned waltz.

Breathless, dizzy, she gave herself up to that dance. She could not do otherwise with Michael's arm around her. He was superb on his feet, swift, graceful, agile for such a tall man. He held her very close . . . so close that she could feel the strong measured beats of his heart against her breast. What a dance! What a night! And only sometimes through her intoxicated mind crept the remembrance of Lionel . . . Lionel, to whom she was to be married as soon as she reached

Hungary. Why, *why* couldn't she feel about him as she felt about this Michael . . . a strange, mad excitement like a fever running through her veins? That was how a woman should feel about a man. Or was she just bewitched? She neither knew nor cared.

For half an hour she danced with Michael. When the music ceased, he let go of her. His face looked suddenly pale in the unearthly light of the moon. He said:

'You're *too* lovely! I wonder if you know how you look with that gorgeous red hair of yours tumbling about your face! It's like a fire. It burns away men's sanity . . . your lovely hair. Do you know that?'

She could not answer, but she thought it high time she said good night to this man. Was he a man or a devil to say and do such things? It was not fair on any girl with the breath of romance in her body. She just turned, quite blindly, and ran away from him downstairs. As she opened her cabin door she felt something hurt her finger. It was her engagement ring . . . the big square-cut diamond which Lionel had sent her as soon as she had promised to marry him. Had Michael noticed it? If so, he had not mentioned the fact. But lots of women wore a ring on that finger and it did not necessarily mean an engagement. She knew suddenly that she did not want Michael to look upon her as a girl affianced to another man. For the second time that day she made a mad, impulsive decision. She took the ring from her finger and locked it in her dressing-bag. And she had no intention of putting it on again tomorrow morning.

2

Morning came. Rina had slept soundly, and she rose early to find the sun pouring in through the porthole. It was a hot, glorious day. She put on a thin blue linen dress and, leaving her head uncovered, walked up on deck.

The barge was well down the river now. The water was a transparent, shining green. There were dark green forests along the shore and more fairy castles, silhouetted against the blue sky.

'How beautiful it all is,' she thought, and found herself wondering if Michael had already been out. She wanted to see him again, to share the beauty of the morning with him, to hear him say her name: '*Rina*' — in that rich, exciting voice. If only she could have felt that way about Lionel! Poor Lionel! She knew that she could never make him really happy. But she was willing to try. And she would have the rest of her life in which to make the effort!

Then she saw Michael, wearing white linen with a gay-coloured scarf around his brown neck, leaning against the rail. He was smoking a cigarette.

She hesitated for a second, then called to him.

'Good morning — Michael!'

At once he turned to her, threw away his cigarette and came eagerly to her side.

'You're up early. Have you had breakfast?'

She shook her head.

'No, I'm only just up.'

'Then let's go down and eat. It seems a shame to miss even a moment of this scenery. But we have all day to appreciate it.'

She followed him down to the little saloon where they were welcomed by a smiling steward. She felt suddenly radiantly happy and realized that this unusual man was the cause of her sudden gaiety, but she refused to admit to herself that she was doing wrong. Her future promised to be flat and dull, without a single thrill in it. But these few days on the barge could be glorious. The evenings — if like last night — would be more than glorious. Why shouldn't she have one memory to take through life with her? Just one!

Into her mind came the amusing thought of that dance-tune which had been so popular in England. It was so applicable — although the wrong river was mentioned.

Thanks for the memory . . .
Of castles on the Rhine
Of candlelight and wine
How lovely it was!

Well, this would be lovely, too.
The same thought was in her mind through the day — a day spent at Michael's side. It served as an excuse for herself when she allowed him to think that there was no question of her being engaged, or about to be married.

They were grand friends during that golden, lazy day — just as they had been last night — while the barge drifted down towards Hungary. Michael knew the route by heart. He pointed out the most famous of the lovely old castles, told her their names, spoke to her of the beauty, the deathless romance and charm of old Hungary. But he never spoke about himself, nor questioned her about her own life. Only once he said:

'You are wise, Rina, to like freedom, as I do. It is the only way to live. When you are staying with your friends, we must meet again.'

She had no answer for that, but felt troubled and guilty. Gradually into her heart crept a feeling of bitter regret. Less than ever she wished to marry Lionel and shut herself away from everything — from life such as she was living it now. This man was drawing her towards him. She grew more conscious of that hour by hour until at last she felt that whither he went, she must go.

Deliberately she placed herself in his

path during the rest of the voyage. They were seldom apart. And then the last night came. At dawn they were due at the river harbour of Budapest.

The closer they came to their destination, the more sensible was Rina of a queer desperation — a feeling approaching panic in her very soul. But Michael seemed elated.

'Hungary will seem a different place now that you are in it,' he told her.

Those words made her heart leap.

So this adventure was to end in something real — and serious. Then she felt sunk — hopeless. No — it must not be serious. She must tell him soon that she was engaged to Lionel — that she had come out here to marry Lionel.

She kept putting off the moment of confession. She snatched at the last few crumbs of happiness. She had only just learned what it meant to be really happy — that was when she was with *him*.

That night they sat together on deck in the warm starlight. Rina looked at the stern, strong profile of the man who fascinated her so strangely, and a shiver of fear passed through her body at the thought of tomorrow, when she must part from him — for ever.

'Are you cold, Rina?' he asked anxiously.

'No,' she said.

He brought a rug and wrapped it about her knees. She felt his warm hand touch her. He said:

'You *are* cold . . . '

'Not really.'

He turned his attention for a moment to the river.

'In Hungarian water now, Rina — well . . . tomorrow — is it to be goodbye? We have been such grand friends. It was a marvellous thing — meeting you like this.'

Rina tried to force herself to speak, to tell him the truth. But she seemed powerless to say a word about Lionel. Michael had cast a spell over her, a spell which she had no wish to break.

She knew now, definitely, that she

was doing wrong. No longer could she cheat herself into thinking that she had acted decently. She had deceived him and she had walked deliberately into the position in which she now found herself. Her only excuse was that she had been impelled by something stronger than herself.

Michael was attracted by her. She knew it — more than ordinarily attracted. She knew it by every woman's instinct. And she had not the strength of will to ignore what lay in his eyes, in the fine, sensitive curve of his lips. She sat motionless, staring at the river. Then she heard him speak. His head was close to hers.

'Rina . . . how lovely you look in this moonlight. Your hair is like rich red wine when the moon kisses it.'

'Is it?' she said, and laughed a little wildly.

She was frightened to look at him, but gradually he forced her gaze to meet his. His brown face was paler than usual in the brilliant light of the moon.

For a full minute they held that close, devastating gaze. Then he dragged his eyes from her, got up and lit a cigarette. He said with a lightness which he forced:

'Yes. It was your hair I first noticed when I met you. And your eyes. But I'm talking too much — you and the Danube are bewitching me. I'd better say good night.'

'Good night, Michael,' she said, and held out her hand.

He took the small slim hand and held it for a moment, then touched it with his lips. He found it fragrant — intoxicating, and wondered what perfume she used.

'I guess I'm just a little crazy tonight,' he said. 'I'll see you in the morning and help you with your luggage.'

He walked away, and a moment later she saw that he had stopped at the other end of the barge. She covered her face with her hands. She realized that she must let him go, that she must never, never see him again after tomorrow. He had said that he was crazy, but she also was crazy — if anything, madder than he.

Then she heard him singing. She could just hear the words of a song which he had sung to her last night, a plaintive Hungarian melody. He had translated the words for her, and she had thrilled to the wild, heart-stirring rhythm.

'You are the heart of me, now.
The breath that I draw,
The wild, passionate breath of my body.
Keep close to me, beloved.
For if you go, you take from me my heart,
And I shall breathe no more
For you will have taken my breath,
Stolen from me my life. So . . .
Keep close to me, beloved,
For without you I die . . . '

Extravagant words, wild, passionate words. Under normal circumstances,

Rina might have laughed at them. When she had looked back at the life she had led in an English village . . . she could see herself laughing at such undue sentimentalism.

But on this barge, drifting down this river, she could not laugh because everything was so abnormal and seemed so tremendous . . . out of proportion, perhaps, but of colossal importance, all the same. And of stirring and vivid reality.

'Stay close to me . . . for without you I die.'

Was that the way Michael would feel about a woman whom he loved? She could imagine a woman feeling like that about *him*.

Oh God, Rina thought, why had she ever allowed herself to reach this pitch? For the first time she was mortally afraid of herself and of her feelings, and she regretted not having gone straight to Budapest by train.

She stood up and let the rug fall from

her knees. She must go to her cabin, to bed; leave this thing alone. She must get off the barge first thing in the morning, when they touched Budapest.

She knew now that she loved this mysterious stranger who called himself Michael; that she was desperately in love for the first time in her life. And she must hurt him — and herself. If she left in the morning without any explanation it would hurt him as much as if she told him now, and be more cowardly. She had better go to him tonight, explain and ask his forgiveness.

She went towards Michael. He was still leaning over the rail, with a cigarette between his fingers as she had seen him that first night on the barge, when one look from his eyes had thrilled her heart.

'Don't go on singing,' she said wildly.

He turned to her, astonished.

'Rina! But why?'

'Because I can't stand it.'

He laughed, the low, rich laugh which she had learned to love. Then,

34

taking her in his arms, he pulled her towards him. He held her fiercely against his body as if fearful that she might escape. The restraint of the last hours was forgotten. He was a man in love, with the woman he loved in his arms.

'Rina,' he whispered. 'My beautiful Rina. The woman whom I love — the only woman whom I will ever love.'

For a moment she tried to hold him back, to speak.

'No, Michael. Wait . . . '

'You know I love you,' he said, as if unconscious of her words. 'You know that I fell in love with you when I first saw you standing on this barge. Now there will be no goodbye. This is only the beginning — for us both.'

She closed her eyes, struggling for sanity. It was all too plain to her that this was love, the wild, obliterating love of her dreams. She loved this man whom she had only met a few short hours ago — she would always love him. But she must force herself to remember Lionel, to tell Michael the truth.

'Michael,' she said wildly. 'Don't kiss me, please! Wait, you must know something that I . . . '

'That you what?' he said, looking down at her. 'What is it that I must know, my darling?'

'That I — I'm not free to love you.'

For a moment he continued to hold her against him, then she felt his arms release her. His expression changed. The light faded in his eyes.

'You're not free? What do you mean by 'not free'? Are you married?'

Rina made an effort. The words which she forced from her lips became stumbling, disjointed sentences. She told Michael of the future life which she must lead in Hungary. She spoke of the romantic dreams which she had woven as a child; of her determination to grab at the last few moments of life which had been offered to her. He, Michael, had given her a taste of the first real happiness she had ever known, she said.

She would be grateful to him; remember him always — if only he would tell her that he was not hurt, if only he would try to understand, to forgive her.

'Please, Michael,' she asked, clinging to his arm, '*try* to understand. I didn't want to hurt you — to hurt myself. I was merely groping wildly for everything which must be denied me. I knew all the time that I was being a fool, but it was too strong for me. I was lost from the moment I spoke to you on board.'

Michael stood back and looked over her head towards the river. For a moment she thought he was going to leave her there without a word. Then he spoke without looking at her. His voice was flat and cold.

'Don't apologize, my dear. I am the one who should apologize — not to you — to your unknown *fiancé*. But I warn you that you can't do this sort of thing in Hungary. It's as well you know that before you land.'

'What do you mean?' she asked. She felt dead, emotionless now, conscious only of obliterating shame.

'That the Hungarians are a lawless people,' he said. 'But that they have a code which, first and foremost, stands for honour and decency — and they expect their women to share it.'

The words whipped the colour to her cheeks. But there was nothing she could say. She would willingly bury her pride, listen to anything he might say about her, if only she could make him understand.

'I know what you must feel about me, Michael. But for God's sake try — '

She broke off and began to weep uncontrollably. He shrugged his shoulders. He seemed utterly unmoved by her grief, her distress.

'You'd better get a grip on yourself, my dear. You'll want to look your best tomorrow, and, personally, I'm afraid I'm still sufficiently English to abhor a scene. And apparently sufficient of an Englishman to let the Danube and the moon make a damned fool of me — goodbye.'

He turned on his heel and moved away.

Rina leaned against the rail and buried her face in her hands. It was finished. Her dream had turned into a hideous nightmare. She would never see him again, this mysterious, attractive Michael. Never hear that low, haunting laugh of his again. Never again know the delirium of his embrace. And she would never be able to forget. The memory of these golden days and unearthly nights on the Danube would always be with her. All her life she would remember that one breathless kiss, the moment when she was in the arms of the only man whom she could ever love.

Mechanically, and with a feeling of complete futility, she walked to her cabin and began to pack for the morning's journey.

The next day revealed to Rina the Hungary which she had so often heard described by Lionel. The great mountains. The Quest's castle — a magnificent grey pile, with battlements and towers pointing upwards to the aching blue sky, silhouetted against those jagged mighty mountains which were crested white with the eternal snows.

Never before had she seen such beauty, such wild and splendid scenery as she looked upon from the tall, narrow windows of her bedroom. A huge, luxurious room with all the modern comforts that money could buy, and which breathed of London and Paris. The walls were panelled in old, shining oak. There were rich Persian rugs on a parquet floor, the latest radio-gramophone, a great double bed on a dais with an amber silk canopy and golden spread. Flowers, books, everything she could desire. A royal room, Rina told herself, fit for a queen.

Indeed, Rina had only been there a few hours before she realized that as Lionel's wife she would be, virtually, a queen. His means obviously unlimited; his power seemed equally so. Here was the last of the feudal system. The people in the territory for miles around, mostly Magyar peasants and gypsies, were his tenants. The castle was full of servants, who wore a green uniform with the crest of the Quests. Rina found herself being treated with almost embarrassing deference.

All that day she had determined to dismiss the agony of last night from her mind — to forget Michael. But her thoughts had been full of him rather than of this exotic, romantic castle. Her brain was haunted by memories of their brief, lovely romance with its bitter ending.

Where was he now? Where did he live? She had not set eyes on him since he had left her on board the barge. Before she disembarked she had looked for him, but he had disappeared. Finally the little Austrian steward told her that the Excellency had left at an early hour that morning, when they had first touched the harbour at Budapest.

So she had gone, miserably, to an hotel and telephoned to her *fiancé*. He at once sent his car for her. She had been brought up to the mountains and found that his mother had recovered and that he, himself, was in excellent spirits. She was received by them both with great enthusiasm. He did not complain because she had come from Vienna by water. It was good for her to see the country, he had said.

He was charming to her, considerate of her every wish, which seemed to Rina to make the position even more difficult. And his mother, although a proud, cold woman, was gracious and friendly to her future daughter-in-law.

Tomorrow they were to be married. Already the village of Foracza was *en fête*. Tonight the Castle grounds would be illuminated. There were to be fireworks, and the Magyar gypsies from the surrounding country would come to dance their lovedance in honour of their lord's wedding to the English lady.

Rina looked from her bedroom window towards the snow-water which, thawed by the hot Hungarian sunshine, rushed in a cascade from the peaks, close to the castle walls.

It was unbelievably lovely. If she had not met Michael, she might have been thrilled; able to settle down here in the castle with some ultimate chance of contentment. But those days on the barge, and the memory of Michael, spoilt any hope of happiness for her.

Later that night when she went down to dinner she was looking her loveliest. She wore a dress of parchment-coloured satin which touched the tips of her small shoes. Her red curls were touched to molten gold in the light of the great silver candelabra, which gleamed throughout the castle. Madame Quest disliked electric light.

Lionel was waiting for Rina in the hall; a magnificent room, its stone floor covered with rich rugs; walls hung with priceless Flemish tapestries. The diamond-paned windows were open to the night. The brocaded curtains had not yet been drawn.

'You look like a princess in that dress,

43

Rina,' he said, taking her hand. 'A fitting princess for my castle home.'

'You're very kind, Lionel,' she said.

He *was* kind — embarrassingly so. Before he took her in to dinner he gave her a present which he had bought for her in Vienna on his way home from England. A rope of superbly graded pearls. As he fastened them around her neck, he bent to kiss her lips.

'The next present I give,' he said, 'will be to my wife — tomorrow.'

Rina felt her cheeks flush with a sudden anger. She hated Lionel when he was possessive. His arrogant, haughty manner infuriated her. When he kissed her, his lips were eager. They grew more eager with every kiss. And tomorrow she would be his wife. She wondered if she could bear it, if it would not be better to make a last-minute bid for freedom.

To Rina the dinner seemed interminable, but Lionel was more than usually cheerful and entertaining. If he noticed that she was silent and thoughtful, that she ate and drank little, he did not mention it. Only when they were alone together, after the meal, did he speak to her about herself.

'You look tired, my darling,' he said. 'These celebrations will probably go on most of the night, but you shouldn't stay up too long.'

'I'm all right, Lionel,' she smiled. 'Just a bit of a headache. I'll go and get some air on the terrace while you finish your cigar. If I don't feel better I'll go straight to my room in a few moments' time.'

Throwing a short fur cape over her bare shoulders, she walked through the open french windows into the Castle grounds. The flare of torches lit up the terraces. The peasants were pouring in a steady stream towards the gardens. She could hear the murmur of excited voices as they jostled each other to get settled in the best positions in order to watch the festivities. Then a rocket soared into the sky, burst and fell in a golden shower of sparks above her head.

Rina walked slowly towards a clump of trees at the other end of the grounds. She wanted to get away from the crowd, to regain some degree of control before she must return to Lionel.

Suddenly she heard a man's voice close beside her. For a moment she was startled as she saw the figure of a gypsy in front of her. He was a tall, gaunt man wearing the traditional gold ear-rings and red sash of his tribe. Quickening her pace, she turned back towards the lights of the house, only to find that another figure had come out of the shadow of the trees to bar her progress.

The memory of the next few moments was a mixture of fear and horror. She knew that she screamed, that her cry for help was lost in a burst of Tzigane music from the terrace, that she tried to bite the hand which was clapped over her mouth. She remembered being carried through some woods until they came to the roadway, where four mountain ponies stood beside another gypsy. She heard muffled whisperings while they tied her arms and legs and gagged her mouth. Then the first man mounted and she was pulled into the saddle in front of him.

She could see, but neither move nor speak. From her uncomfortable position in the saddle, held by the gypsy's arm, she saw that they were galloping down a narrow, dusty road, away from the lights of Foracza, towards the mountains. Reaching a narrow bridle-path, they began to climb. Steadily, persistently, they climbed, until it seemed to Rina that they must reach the very stars.

She made an effort to think clearly, but her brain, numb with terror and fear, refused to act. Already the towers and battlements of the Castle below them were out of sight. Gradually the lights of the village vanished. But she could still hear the occasional sound of music, see the bursting of the rockets. The festivities in celebration of her wedding-eve were in full swing.

What would Lionel do? It could not be long before he found that she had disappeared. Surely with his powers and resources it must be a matter of hours before she was traced and rescued? It seemed incredible, even in a country like Hungary with its admittedly lawless element, that she should be spirited away from the grounds of her *fiancé's* own home.

By the time that long climb ended, Rina was feeling sick with fear. What did they mean to do with her? Probably hold her for ransom. In that case, of course, Lionel would pay without question. She was convinced that he would go to any length to get her back in time for their wedding.

She saw now that they had reached a plateau in the mountains, a shelf on the rock from which had been hewn out the entrance to a network of caves. They were, she realized, approaching one of these Magyar encampments of which she had heard Lionel and his mother speak.

The ponies stopped — the gypsy jumped from the saddle and helped Rina to the ground. He untied her hands and feet and removed the gag from her mouth. He signed to her to follow him. Rina went helplessly towards the caves. It was useless to try to argue, she could see that; to make any demonstration with these people who could not even understand what she said. She must try to keep calm, to control herself, and realize that Lionel would soon send help.

The gypsy led her to one of the caves and, without speaking, pushed her in and bolted the door behind her. Rina stared about her. Curiosity mingled with fear now. This place could not belong to one of the ragged men who had brought her. It was almost luxurious. An oil-lamp swung on silver chains from the vaulted roof; the walls were hung with rich-coloured rugs, which stood out warmly against the grey stone. The mosaic floor was covered with a Chinese carpet. All stolen goods, she supposed. In one corner stood a carved table, of cedar-wood, and next to it a divan covered with Hungarian embroideries and great silk cushions.

Rina decided that this was the dwelling-place of the tribe. Probably some man like the famous Miska whom Lionel had spoken to her about.

She began to recall the fantastic story of the elusive Magyar chief. Lionel had been telling her that afternoon about him and of the efforts which had been made to bring him to heel. Miska was a clever outlaw and was always missing when they raided his mountain hide-outs. The Hungarian police were unable, by bribes or threats, to get any information from his followers. His people were loyal and the man continued to lead his life unhampered by the law at which he openly sneered.

Rina shivered and drew her fur cape closer about her. If this was Miska's work, perhaps neither Lionel nor the police would ever trace her. She began to walk up and down the cave. She felt cold and stiff after the long journey on the pony. Yet it was quite warm in the cave. An oil-stove was burning at the far end.

Suddenly she stopped and turned. The door had creaked on its hinges. A woman entered, an old white-haired woman with dangling ear-rings which swung against her wizened face. In her hand she carried a bowl of steaming soup.

'For you,' she said in tolerable English.

Rina seized her arm.

'You speak English?' she cried. 'Thank God for that. Tell me where I am — why I've been brought here.'

The old woman regarded her curiously.

'This is the cave of Miska, in highest peak of Svita mountains.'

'But why am I here?'

'Brought for Miska.'

Rina clung to the woman's arm.

'*Brought for him!* What on earth are you talking about? What do you mean, '*brought for him*'?'

The woman regarded her almost scornfully.

'Miska great man — our leader. You English woman to be his bride.'

'His bride!' Rina echoed the words dazedly. 'For God's sake talk sensibly. Why do you say anything so fantastic? Let me see this man Miska — let me speak to him.'

'He come to you at midnight,' the woman said quietly. 'He tells me to give you this soup, that you should prepare to receive him.'

Rina laughed hysterically as the woman left, closing the door behind her. The whole thing was too incredible to be true. It was a fairy-tale. A film. A silly story. Or she must wake up soon to find that it was all a nightmare. Gypsy outlaws — caves in mountains! Bride of Miska, whom Lionel had said was the most 'wanted' man in Hungary! The situation was too fantastic.

Lighting a cigarette, she began once again to walk round the cave. She wondered when they would tell Lionel. Perhaps they had already demanded the ransom money! In that case, they might let her go tonight or in the morning. The old woman's story of Miska's bride was obviously rubbish. The only thing these people would take such a risk for must be money.

She looked at the watch on her wrist. It was three minutes to twelve. When this gypsy, Miska, came . . . please God he could speak English . . . she would tell him that the Quests would pay; she would try to persuade him to let her return that night.

He arrived on the stroke of midnight. Rina, hearing footsteps, tried to control the pounding of her heart. She was near to fainting when at length the door opened and the gypsy entered the cave. He was Miska the outlaw, dressed in national costume — a gaily embroidered white blouse, dark velvet breeches, a scarlet sash around his waist, a wide-brimmed hat on his head. In his sash was a jewelled dagger, and he carried a rifle in his hand.

Rina stared up at him. So this was Miska — the gypsy king! Jumping to her feet with a cry, she drew a hand across her eyes. It was impossible! The final, incredible turn in this grotesque dream! Yet it *was* real! It was the same proud, thin face; the same unforgettable grey eyes; the same man whom she had learned to love on the barge.

'Michael!' she sobbed. '*Michael!*'

For a moment he stood looking down at her, then, leaning the rifle against the wall, he sat on the edge of the table.

'No,' he said, shaking his head, ''*Miska*'. In Vienna, on the barge, I was Michael. Here, in my home, amongst my people. I am Miska — the gipsy.'

Rina fought for self-control. She wanted to be proud; to hide from the fear which she felt. Fear mingled with wild relief at the sight of him.

'But, Michael,' she protested, 'tell me what all this means — why you have brought me here! You must know that my people — the police — will find out;

that they will never stop searching until I return. It can only be a matter of time until they trace me. You must be mad!'

He flung back his head and laughed.

'Perhaps I am. But don't worry about the police. They've been trying to find me for years and there's no reason why they should do so now.'

'But why did you bring me here?' she repeated wildly.

He took a cigarette from his case and lit it by the light of the oil-lamp.

'On the barge,' he said, speaking slowly, 'I told you that I refused to be hide-bound by convention and that I did not believe in the laws of modern society. I also told you that I had definite ideas about a woman's sense of decency and honour. You cheated me on that barge. You took off your ring, led me to believe you were free and — '

'I know, I know,' she broke in; 'but what has all that got to do with this business?'

'Nothing,' he smiled, 'except that I happened to fall in love with you.'

55

She swallowed hard, her heart still pounding.

'But you know it's hopeless — that I'm going to marry someone else.'

'I know that you came out to be married to some fellow. You told me so on the barge — too late. If you hadn't tricked me those first two days, this position would not have arisen. As a rule I steer clear of other men's women.'

'Are you so strictly honourable?' she said, with some irony.

He nodded.

'In such a case — yes. A man and woman should start squarely — which we did not do.'

Now she was afraid of him, realizing dimly that he had it in his power to dictate, to keep her here. Her one idea was to escape, to get away. Yet she loved him completely, must always love him. With a sudden spasm of fear, she watched him. She saw that he was smiling to himself.

She said desperately:

'If you've got such ideas of honour, why take me away now — from my fiancé?'

He rose to his feet and looked down at her.

'I'm sure you must be wondering that. Well, I'll tell you.' He came close to her, so close that she could feel his breath upon her hair, hear his quick breathing. 'When I said goodbye to you on the barge, I meant it. I never intended to see you again. I had learned, in those short days, to love you. Then you told me the truth and I hated you — and desired you — at the same time. But I put you out of my life. So far as I was concerned, the episode was closed.'

'I know, Michael,' she said. 'I know I behaved rottenly. But you must see that this can only make things more impossible — for us both. You know I'm marrying Lionel Quest, you know his power in this country. If you hold me here, it must only be a matter of hours before he finds me.'

Michael spun round on his heel, and for the first time there was a hard, bitter ring in his voice.

'Like hell it will!' he said savagely. 'Lionel Quest has been hunting me for years. He won't get me now. If you'd been going to marry any other man, you wouldn't have been here.'

Rina stared at him blankly.

'I don't understand.'

'Of course you don't,' he told her, with a bitter laugh. 'You don't know of the injustice and cruelty which he perpetrated on me and on my people. But it happens to rankle in my mind. I vowed vengeance and I have waited to take it. You put it into my hands.'

'I did . . . ?'

He flung back his head and laughed.

'Of course you did, my dear Rina. I would have left you alone if you had been about to marry *any other man on earth*. But Lionel Quest is my enemy and I must live up to my reputation. The reputation of Miska the Gypsy. Miska takes what he wants. I have taken you — from Quest. *I want you, Rina. And I want to hurt Quest.* So, tonight, you lie in my arms. Tonight shall be one night of love — for you — for me. Tomorrow — you shall be returned — to Lionel Quest.'

She looked up at the impassioned stormy face of the man and tried to laugh, but the laughter died in her throat. His eyes terrified her. She realized now that she had never known the real Michael. The sensitive, understanding companion of the barge was the very antithesis of the gypsy who stood before her. She said breathlessly:

'You can't do this to me. You dare not.'

She regretted her words as soon as they were spoken.

'There is nothing which Miska does not dare do,' he answered harshly. 'You don't seem to understand that — yet.'

'But you aren't really a gypsy. You're English.'

'Forget that, Rina. It is best forgotten. Remember that I am Miska, the

59

king of the mountains, and that you once made a fool of the king.'

'Was it *all* my fault?'

He folded his arms across his chest and looked at her through narrowed eyes.

'Yes, all your fault. I would not have stayed by your side day and night had I known you were coming out here to marry Lionel Quest.'

'Why do you hate him so?' she asked. 'What has he done to you?'

'That is my affair,' he said roughly. 'You need only concern yourself with this — you will belong to *me*, before you marry *him*.'

They stood looking at each other. His determination appalled her. She was frantic with fear.

'You must let me go,' she said in a choked voice. 'Tell them to set me free, take me back.'

'You shall go back — tomorrow,' he said. 'Not until then.'

'Michael — '

'I am Miska the Gypsy,' he broke in.

'Cease to think of me as your English friend and companion of those days and nights on the river. I had illusions about you then, Rina. I respected and admired you. Tonight I only *want you* . . . I know neither admiration nor respect.'

In spite of the terror which clutched at her heart, Rina was conscious of an ever-growing wave of anger against this man who was so calmly dictating his demands. She knew that she had injured him. She had already admitted that her conduct on the barge had been cruel, that she had hurt him unnecessarily. But no wrong which she had done could merit his present attitude. He could not treat her as he would one of his uncivilized camp-followers whom he wished to punish for some crime.

'Listen, Michael,' she said. 'You seem to think you can order me about like these gypsies. But you're wrong. I've told you that I regret the episode on the barge. I've apologized. I can do no more.'

'You can do a lot more,' he said, making a sudden movement towards her. 'You can kiss me now, and tonight you can lie in my arms and be glad that you have discovered what love *can* mean.'

Rina felt his strong hands on her shoulders as he bent to kiss her. It was impossible to get away from him. She was trapped. But the anger which had been smouldering in her heart was fanned by every kiss which burnt on her lips. She was not frightened now, only conscious of the fact that he had humiliated her. She was furiously angry. She told herself that never while there was breath in her body would she submit to him.

Drifting down the Danube on the barge, when she had listened to his rich voice, she had learned to love him desperately. But passion walks hand in hand with hatred, and hatred gleamed out of Rina's eyes now as she tried to free herself from his arms.

'You cad!' she said, pushing him

violently away from her. 'You utter brute!'

Michael let her go, and standing back looked down into her flashing eyes.

'I like you when you're angry,' he said. 'It pleases me. But remember that you have roused the devil in me. I despise women who pretend to be free and then laugh as you must have done, once you were with Lionel Quest.'

'I didn't laugh,' Rina began, but stopped, choking. No, never would she give this man the satisfaction of knowing how she regretted what she had done. She would never tell him how bitterly she had wanted him, how she had ached for those glorious days and nights again.

'Don't let us waste time,' Michael said, ignoring her words. 'Tonight you are mine, Rina. The night is short — so let us make the best of it.'

Suddenly she ran towards the door of the cave; but Michael, stepping neatly in front of her, stood with one black eyebrow raised in insolent appraisal of her beauty.

'Don't hurry, Rina,' he laughed. 'When you leave, it will be in my arms.'

Once again her temper flared. She stamped a small foot.

'You fool!' she cried. 'Lionel will make you pay for this.'

Michael's face changed. The laughter died in his eyes.

'Will he? Well, first of all he will suffer — the loss of his beautiful, innocent bride. When you return to him, Rina, the seal of Miska's love will be stamped upon you, never to be erased.'

'*Miska's love!*' she repeated bitterly. 'You call this playacting 'love'?'

He smiled strangely and clapped his hands. At once the door opened and the old gypsy woman came in, carrying a silver goblet of red wine. Handing it to Miska, she left silently, closing the heavy oak door behind her.

'Our loving cup,' Michael said. 'Drink, Rina . . . '

'No!'

'Listen to me,' he said harshly. 'This is our marriage wine — according to our Magyar customs. Drink it and you will want my love even more than you did on the barge. You *remember* how you felt then! You came when I called, went where I went. You wanted me for your lover, those starry nights on the Danube — you wanted my love — didn't you? Answer me!'

She tried to get away from him.

'I won't answer you. I loathe you now — whatever happened on the barge.'

He put the cup down, lifted her off her feet and kissed her on the lips; kissed her until she was spent and exhausted. Threading his fingers through her hair, he bent her head back and brushed his lips against her throat.

Rina felt that she had no fight left. She was half-fainting when he let her go. Leaning back against the wall, she shut her eyes, one shaking hand against her mouth.

Miska looked at her. She was wonderfully beautiful in that parchment-coloured dress, standing against the rich red and blue of a Persian rug which hung on the wall. Her face was ivory white. He knew that he had hurt her. He thought:

'I have never loved any woman as I love this one. But if I am cruel to her, she deserves it. She was crueller than the grave to me. And tomorrow she must go to Lionel Quest . . . *tomorrow!*'

If he felt the slightest twinge of pity for her, he did not show it. Walking towards her, he held the loving-cup to her lips.

'Will you drink — now? Or shall I kiss you into obedience?'

Rina raised her head and looked into his eyes.

'I prefer to drink.'

He shrugged his shoulders and smiled.

'You are wise, my Rina!'

She took the goblet and drank thirstily, hoping that the wine would give her strength to face the next hours. When it was finished, she threw down the glass.

'I hate you!' she cried as it smashed on the floor. 'God only knows how I hate you!'

'Forget that,' he said quietly. 'Just remember that tonight belongs to us.'

He had swung now from ruthless cruelty to tender passion. He dried the tears which she was trying to keep back, smiled into her eyes as he had done that first night on the Danube.

Gradually the flame of battle died down in her soul. She felt the wine warm her aching limbs. It seemed to give her courage. Certainly this gypsy loving-cup was instantaneous and striking in its effect. It dulled her memory, prevented clear thought, yet her limbs felt strong and capable.

A moment later she found herself walking out of the cave, hand in hand with Michael — walking straight, upright, unafraid. But she could not think. Everything was blurred. The past and present merged into each other. She walked as though in a dream, a trance, and the rest of the happenings of that night passed as in a picture before her — a changing kaleidoscope of colour.

On the mountain plateau the gypsies had lit a fire. In vast crowds they walked around it, each man with a torch in his hand. A great white moon hung in the starlit sky. A thousand feet below lay Foracza — out of sight.

The men, like their leader, wore brightly embroidered Hungarian blouses and velvet breeches. The women, thick striped shirts, heavy gold ear-rings dangling against their handsome dusky cheeks.

They trooped round Michael and Rina, smiling reverently but without shyness, and began to sing. Their music was gay, their voices fresh and clear as the stream which ran down the mountain to the valley.

Michael led Rina towards a dais which had been prepared for them; the eyes of the crowd following their every movement. This was a woman worthy of their own Miska. A slender beautiful woman — a lily, with her fair skin — a princess from a fairy castle, stolen by her gypsy lover.

Rina sank on to a stool and clasped her hands about her knees. She looked dreamily on the scene before her. No longer did she care what happened to her. She did not argue with Michael or protest. Her brain was cloudy. Only her senses were acute, stirred by the rich colours, the warm starlight, the sound of the wild Hungarian rhythm played by the musicians.

Michael watched her, his grey eyes brooding. He knew that the wine was taking effect on her. If she sat still she would drift into a state of indifference and apathy. He rose suddenly and caught her round the waist.

'You shall dance with me,' he said, 'the Magyar lovedance.'

The watching gypsies broke into cheering when they saw their beloved leader take his woman in his arms. They watched him whirl Rina into a crowd of dancers, watched the revolving figures move wildly to the passionate throb of violin strings. The fire blazed, the torches were shooting golden sparks high into the night.

Rina, crushed against Michael's body, ceased to think, but her blood ran fiercely through her veins as the wine took further effect.

When that wild dance ended, she remembered him saying with his lips against her ear:

'So you love me again, my Rina?'

And she, looking up to his face, had answered:

'Michael . . . kiss me . . . '

'It is Miska who kisses you — who makes you his bride by gypsy law,' she heard his rich, compelling voice tell her. 'Mine, Rina . . . for ever . . . '

'Miska's woman — by gypsy law!' thundered a thousand voices in the Magyar tongue.

She did not know what they said, but later another hazy remembrance came to her of being carried in Michael's strong arms away from the wild scene of dancing and music, away from the glare of the fire and the torches, back to the solitary splendour of his cave.

For a brief moment, when he laid her on the gaily coloured divan by the dim light of a single silver lamp, her subconscious mind stirred — rebelled.

'Let me go,' she murmured. 'Let me go.'

She heard no answer to her words. Only eager arms about her, eager lips against her mouth. She felt herself responding, madly, to that first long kiss. Then there was darkness and silence. She felt detached, peaceful, as if in the middle of a dream.

The last thing she heard, the last recollection of that dream, was a man's passionate, bitter voice which said:

'Rina, my own Rina. I would so gladly have dedicated myself to you. I could have loved you better than life itself . . . Why did you do this thing to me?'

3

Rina awoke to find herself in her own great four-poster bed in the Castle. The warm sunlight was streaming through the windows; birds were singing melodiously in the trees outside the balcony.

She sat up stiffly, putting her hand to her aching head, and looked around her. How did she come to be there? Why was she not up in the mountain cave of Miska the Gypsy?

She wondered if it had not all been a dream, if those hours last night had not all been a strange, fantastic nightmare, if when she was fully awake she would find that she had never left the grounds of the Castle. But as clear thought and memory came back to her, she knew that it was no nightmare. It was a sinister reality.

She saw that she was still wearing her evening dress, that she was lying fully clothed under the embroidered spread.

Who had put her there, covered her? Who had brought her back? Somebody, mysteriously, in the night, before dawn, must have carried her back to the Castle.

Surely it could not all be true . . . ?

Then she saw that a piece of paper, a note, was pinned to the corner of her pillow. Quickly, with shaking fingers, she tore it open. The words were written in pencil in Michael's hand:

You are mine (she read). *The gold chain around your neck makes us one. It is the gypsy token of marriage.*

Miska.

Rina stared at the note, then, putting a hand to her throat, felt the thin chain which encircled her neck. It had no clasp. It must have been sealed round her neck. Sealed by Miska — the seal of their marriage.

Her brain reeled. Then it was true!

She had not fallen asleep and dreamed this thing. She *had* been carried off by gypsies and taken up to the mountains — she *had* been the victim of Miska's vengeance last night.

Pale as the magnolia blossom outside her balcony, Rina staggered to her feet and stared at herself in the mirror. She was a wreck. Her dress was crushed and torn, her hair dishevelled, her eyes shadowed, and her lips seemed still to smart from the mad, fierce kisses of her lover.

Her lover! Rina felt the colour stain her cheeks and throat. Heaven knows she had paid a heavy price for her treatment of Michael on the barge. She belonged to him now, had been made his by every gypsy law and by the law of love.

Rina wrenched savagely at the golden chain around her neck, but it did not break. She wanted to forget Miska and the fantasy of last night. What a fool she had been to drink that wine! If she had refused, she might have had sufficient strength to make him change his mind. But now at least she was safe among civilized people, she could afford to laugh at his wild threats. She would not pay any attention to the thing he had done. She would show him that he was not her master, that she was contemptuous of his so-called 'marriage'.

Taking off her torn dress, Rina rang for her maid and told the girl to run her bath and bring her some black coffee. She knew that she would need all her strength before she must face Lionel. There would be explanations to make about her absence from the festivities of the night before. She must be convincing, hide any trace of last night's craziness from her face.

After she had bathed, she dressed carefully and went downstairs. Lionel was in the library reading a paper. He looked up anxiously as she appeared and hurried to meet her.

'Rina, my dear,' he said, holding out a hand. 'I was just beginning to worry. I told the servants not to disturb you because I knew you must be tired. But if you had been much longer, I was going to send up a message.'

Rina took a cigarette from a silver box on the mantel-piece.

'I'm sorry, Lionel,' she said. 'I owe you an apology, especially for last night. But I felt so tired and ill in the garden that I went straight up to my room. I knew you would understand.'

'Of course I understood,' he said. 'But I can't think why I didn't see you come back. Nobody did. You were missing when the people wanted to dance our Magyar love-dance.'

The Magyar love-dance! Rina felt a shiver pass through her body. It was only a few hours before that she had seen that very dance, she had danced it, herself — in Michael's arms. She wondered if it would be better to tell Lionel the truth, to give him an account of last night's wild, strange episode. But the words would not come. No, never would she tell him about Michael. Never! She would go on with her marriage, she would defy Michael, she would never let Lionel know the truth.

'We'll make up for it tonight, my dear,' she said with a forced little laugh. 'I wish you'd give me a drink, my head still aches a bit.'

Lionel glanced at his *fiancée* with some anxiety. She seemed nervy, distraught, and she looked pale and weary. But as lovely as ever, he thought, and this afternoon she was to be made his wife. Well — there would be plenty of time to look after her then. She would soon forget her 'nerves' and become the gay carefree girl whom he had first met in England.

Lionel had never been an inspired lover. His few love-affairs had been cold, without romance. He wanted Rina for his wife because she was beautiful and young; because she would make an exquisite mistress for his castle and mother for his sons. But he was more concerned with his own feelings than with hers.

'Mind you, I did think you were a

little lacking in affection, my darling,' he said. 'I mean . . . to run away from me on our wedding-eve, without even saying good night.'

She avoided his gaze.

'I'm sorry, Lionel.'

'No matter,' he said. Then, frowning, reached out a hand and touched the gold chain about her throat.

'What's that?' he asked.

Rina moistened her dry lips with her tongue.

'Oh, just a chain of mine.'

'You prefer to wear it — instead of my pearls?'

'Don't be silly, Lionel,' she answered crossly. 'You don't expect me to wear those valuable pearls in the morning?'

He shrugged his shoulders and, crossing the room, poured out a glass of sherry which he brought to her. Rina watched him. His cold, precise manner annoyed her. She felt she might very easily learn to loathe his well-bred good looks, that thin, cruel mouth. He never seemed to her quite human.

Handing her the glass, he put an arm around her shoulder and looked into her eyes.

'My dear,' he said. 'What a strange, undemonstrative little thing you are! Aren't you going to kiss me or say a single word to show me that you love me a bit?'

She stood silent and motionless in the curve of his arm. She realized that he would always leave her unmoved. Never in Lionel's embrace could she be shaken, scorched, terrified, as she had been in the arms of Miska the Gypsy. Her heart beat fast. Then she flung back her head as though silently defying Miska and his warning.

'Of course I have a kiss for you, Lionel. Many kisses. Aren't we to be married today?'

For an instant Lionel was aroused from his habitual coldness. He kissed her red lips eagerly.

'Today, yes, at two o'clock this afternoon, darling. Then you will be utterly mine.'

Rina finished her wine and moved towards the hall. There were many things to attend to before the afternoon.

'If I don't go now, Lionel,' she said, forcing a smile, 'you'll have to wait for me at the altar.'

Preparations for the wedding were going steadily ahead throughout the Castle. No money, no trouble, was being spared to make this wedding worthy of the heir to the Quest fortune. Rina thought that Madame Quest, still delicate after her severe illness, moved about rather like an old witch, with her white hair and ebony stick, giving sharp orders to the countless liveried servants. The Castle was filled with flowers, the great hall was a miracle of roses, lilies, carnations, and glittering wax candles which would eventually be lighted.

Later in the day, after a light lunch, Rina found herself surrounded by her maids, dressing for her wedding. She stood silent and thoughtful when they put on her glorious dress of amber satin, her gold shoes, a coronet of orange blossom on her head, a misty gold veil which fell to the hem of her robe. Her train was embroidered with the coat of arms of the Quests, and spread out on the ground like a great fan of gleaming brocade.

When she was dressed, she walked slowly down the broad staircase to the hall where Madame Quest waited to take her to the church. The old lady looked at her with appraising eyes.

'Beautiful, my child,' she said warmly. 'You look radiant — a worthy bride for my son!'

Rina was inclined to smile. It was all absurdly theatrical to her. Like a scene from a Ruritanian play or film.

'Thank you,' she said to the old lady. 'How long before we must leave?'

'In five minutes,' Madame Quest said, pulling on her gloves. 'Lionel has just gone. The poor boy had to find a new best man at the last minute.'

'A new best man?' Rina repeated.

'Did Captain Lipto not arrive?'

Madame Quest shook her head.

'He has just telephoned. It seems that that troublesome fellow Miska the Gypsy was seen this afternoon. And Captain Lipto, being the head of our police, had to lead the search for him.'

A mist came before Rina's eyes. She heard the old lady's voice as if from a distance.

'You mean the *famous* Miska?' she asked, trying to control her words.

'The *infamous* Miska,' Madame Quest said grimly. 'But don't you worry your pretty head about it. That gypsy has gone too far this time. The village is full of police for the wedding. Captain Lipto says they will get him within an hour.'

Rina felt the colour drain from her face under the golden veil. Her hand, holding a great bouquet of lilies and roses, trembled uncontrollably. If Miska was caught, she knew what it would mean. They would shoot him or shut him up in one of the dungeons underneath the Castle. Perhaps that very night when she must lie in Lionel's arms she would know that they had locked *him* up, within a few yards of her.

If only she could forget, dismiss it from her mind! But she knew now that it was impossible. The memory of last night became nearer, more vivid every moment. All her life she would remember that wild, primitive marriage in the mountain under the cold starlight, the gypsy ring, the thousand torches, the Magyar love-dance and — *Michael*.

Madame Quest was speaking once again, but Rina did not even try to hear what she said, or answer. She only knew that she could not go on, that her body was no longer under her control. She was beyond caring. She could not breathe. Very quietly she slid on to the red carpet and lay there a crumpled golden heap.

When she came back to consciousness, she was lying on a sofa. Lionel was beside her rubbing her cold hands, his eyes anxiously searching her face. His voice swirled above her in a sickening mist of noise. She saw that he was in uniform — a privilege granted to the Quests for the last 200 years. Stars, orders, blue ribbons of honour gleamed on his chest. Beside him a magnificent young Hungarian officer in dress-uniform was trying to put some brandy down her throat.

'Drink this,' said Lionel, taking the glass from his brother officer and holding it against Rina's lips.

She gulped and choked, and began coughing as the spirit seared her throat. Then she swallowed deeply and tried to speak.

'I'm sorry, Lionel,' she whispered. 'I tried not to faint.'

'Don't worry, darling,' he said. 'You'll be all right in a few minutes. Look, here is our doctor to see you!'

The doctor who attended Madame Quest, and was one of the wedding guests, bent down and felt Rina's pulse.

A moment later he turned to Lionel.

'She will be all right, Quest. But not in a few minutes. She is in a state of collapse. She must have complete rest for a few days. You'll have to postpone the wedding until then, I'm afraid.'

The anxious look in Lionel's eyes changed to dismay and consternation.

'Postpone the wedding! But look here . . . it can't be as bad as all that . . . surely later today — '

'My dear fellow,' interrupted the doctor, 'believe me, the young lady is in a state of shock and her condition is such that I wouldn't advise you to put her to any further strain today.'

Madame Quest, leaning heavily on her stick, said:

'But this is most puzzling. She was perfectly all right yesterday and went early to bed. What can have caused such a collapse?'

'Mind you,' put in Lionel, 'she did tell me that she wasn't feeling fit last night and that is why she did not stay out for the dancing.'

Madame Quest shook her head.

'And with everything arranged! What a disappointment.'

Lionel turned from the little group and cast a gloomy look at Rina's figure. His personal disappointment was great, but he made an effort to control it.

Walking across the room to her side, he took one of her hands.

'You'll be all right — don't worry,' he said, with admirable self-control.

Rina was carried to her bed. It was Lionel who carried her through the crowd of anxious guests and servants to her room. When he laid her down, he kissed her hair and whispered:

'Get well soon, my darling — for me!'

Rina did not answer. She lay still with closed eyes. The doctor had given her a sleeping-draught. Her maids she dismissed. She wanted to be by herself to think over the whole situation.

Not until she was quite alone in her luxurious bedroom did her nerve give way. She turned her face to the pillow and cried — tears of sheer anger and fright. Why should Michael have this influence over her? Why should the mere mention of his name take the strength from her body? Her slender fingers pulled wildly at the gold chain about her throat. She must find a file, file it off, destroy it.

Slowly the opiate which she had swallowed took effect. That afternoon she slept heavily. Night had already fallen over the mountains and shrouded the Castle in darkness before she woke again.

It was a lovely night of starlight, but moonless. Silence brooded over the battlements and the flower-filled gardens. The servants had been told that no noise must be heard, and that Miss Rina must not be disturbed. Last night there had been wild scenes of festivity. Tonight, disappointed, the guests and villagers remained at home. But it was hoped that the wedding would take place in a couple of days. The doctor's official bulletin said that the bride was only suffering from temporary collapse 'due to over-excitement'.

At eleven o'clock Rina drank a glass of hot milk which her personal maid brought to her. Lying back on her pillow, she tried once again to sleep. But her mind would not stop working. She could not even rest on the bed. Putting on a velvet house-gown, she began to walk up and down her room, both hands pressed to her aching head.

What was she to do? How could she deal with the situation? If Michael was caught by the police and imprisoned in the Castle, it would be impossible for her to live here, knowing that he was so near. Perhaps she could persuade Lionel to take her away for a long honeymoon. He might even consent to a quiet wedding at home in England. She would not mind where they went so long as they were far from here.

Suddenly she stood still. She stared at one of the windows, her heart leaping to her throat. *A heavy silk curtain was moving*, bulged outwards as though by the wind. *Someone was there* — someone climbing in through the window. Rina opened her lips to scream, then closed them again. Her eyes stared feverishly in front of her.

Then a man in gipsy costume leaped lightly into the room and stood before her, one hand on his hip. He smiled at her.

'I greet you!' he said in the Magyar language.

It was Miska . . .

Rina could neither move nor speak. Dumbfounded, she stared, her whole body tense, one slender hand holding the collar of her house-gown about her throat.

Michael's grey, eagle eyes swept round the room scornfully as though he found it over-luxurious, too sweet with the perfume of flowers. He walked straight up to Rina. His boldness swept away her breath. He said:

'You look quite charming here, my Rina. But I preferred you in my simple cave in the mountains. How are you after last night?'

The blood scorched her cheeks. She stepped backwards.

'You fool, Michael!' she panted. 'You mad fool! Don't you know that the police are searching for you, that they — '

'Of course I do,' he interrupted with a laugh, 'and I'm glad to hear that my safety still concerns you.'

'I'm thinking of myself,' she retorted. 'Haven't you tortured me enough? Must this fantastic thing go on?'

'I came to see my wife.'

'Your wife!' she cried. 'I'm not your wife, thank God!'

'Oh, but you are, Rina . . . '

He smiled coolly, and with a quick gesture pulled her hand away from her throat and fixed his burning gaze upon its whiteness.

'You haven't taken off your wedding-ring yet, I see,' he said, as though amused.

'The chain is coming off tonight. Be sure of that.'

'You are not so loving as the old Rina,' he murmured. 'Come, my sweet. I risk my neck to get here — for your kiss.'

She was in his arms then, caught and held in the fierce, possessive clasp which half thrilled and wholly frightened her. Her throat felt dry. Her eyes shone with fear. His lips were on hers at the moment when she heard a noise outside her door. She strained every nerve to listen. There were footsteps, a man's voice — Lionel's voice.

'Rina!' Lionel called, knocking at the door. 'Let me in. Can you hear me? There's a man in your room. I saw him — a cat-burglar on your balcony just now when I looked out of my window.'

Instantly Michael put a hand over Rina's mouth. She heard his low voice, his quickened breathing against her ear.

'If you betray me, Rina, if you call him in, *I swear I will kill him*.'

She looked up into his eyes. They were the eyes of a fighter at bay — deadly, flint-like, ominous. Not the eyes of a man to be trifled with.

Then once again there was knocking at the door.

'Rina. *Rina!* Open your door . . . '

Michael shook the girl in his arms.

'Answer him — tell him to go away,' he whispered.

She forced herself to obey.

'My dear Lionel — what is all this about?' Her voice sounded weak, fretful. 'Nobody is in my room. I am ill, as you know, and trying to sleep.'

Lionel's voice came back, hesitant, doubtful.

'But, my dear, I saw a figure climbing — '

'You saw a shadow from the moon,' she told him. 'Nobody is near my room, otherwise I would have called you. Good night, my dear.'

'Good night,' he said. 'Forgive me — I really thought . . . '

'It was sweet of you,' she answered wearily. 'Good night.'

Lionel made another apology and moved away. They heard his footsteps in the corridor. Rina bit fiercely at her lip. Michael had forced her to send Lionel away. How she hated this man's power, rebelled against his arms which still held her, imprisoning her like a vice.

He was smiling sardonically.

'Beautifully acted, my dear. As good as the show you put up for me on the barge.'

Her eyes flashed. She struggled to release herself from him.

'Let me go.'

His only answer was to laugh, to kiss her hair, her lips. His fingers played with the chain about her neck.

'That binds you to me for ever, Rina,' he said, and this time he was not smiling. He was stern and compelling. 'We shall meet again — soon. Good night, *my* Rina . . . '

He picked her up wholly in his arms and laid her on her golden bed. Then, as she lay there panting, weeping, defeated, he vanished, clambering like a tiger stealthily, without making a sound, clinging to the thick ivy which trailed from Rina's balcony over the grey old walls of the Castle, down to the darkened garden.

Rina rushed to the balcony and leaned over. But Miska had gone. She returned to her bedroom, her face pale with fear and anger. Every nerve in her body ached and quivered, the body he had held so tightly, caressed so passionately.

For a moment she stared at her reflection in the mirror — a pale, angry, tear-wet young face. Then searching in the drawer of her dressing-table she found a small nail-file. Feverishly she began filing at the chain about her neck. But it was hopeless. The file merely glanced off without making any impression.

Suddenly, with a feeling of complete despair, Rina flung the file across the room and, throwing herself face downwards on the bed, broke into uncontrolled tears.

4

In Lionel's oak-panelled study an argument was taking place between the master of the Castle and a short, sturdily built man with a neatly trimmed beard and smooth black hair. The man was in evening dress, but wore a black velvet smoking-jacket instead of the conventional coat.

'You are crazy, Lionel, to be so deceived,' he was saying hotly. 'I tell you I saw him with my own eyes, two minutes ago. A man running across the lawn from the Castle.'

'A thief, no doubt. The one I saw climbing up the ivy. He was frightened and sheered off,' Lionel said. He sat at a table in his dressing-gown, his fingers playing with a revolver. 'Rina convinced me that there was nobody near her room.'

'You are so sure of your *fiancée's* loyalty?'

Lionel leapt to his feet.

'Yes, damn you, Hannen — I *am* sure! Now clear out and don't annoy me with any more of your absurd suspicions.'

Hannen Vaile smiled, a cold, deadly little smile. His lips, full and red against his black Vandyke beard, were sneering. Lionel was a fool to be sure of the beautiful, red-haired Rina.

Vaile was not so certain of her. He suspected, seriously, that she was intriguing behind Lionel's back. He had not mentioned the name to Lionel, but he felt convinced that the man in question was Miska the Gypsy. Vaile had agents abroad in Hungary; men and women who had hinted to him that it was with the notorious Miska that the lovely Rina had spent the hours when she was expected to be present at her wedding celebrations.

Hannen Vaile only wanted to be certain of his facts, to be sure of proving something against her. If there was anybody on earth he disliked — it was this English girl. Her beauty left him unmoved. He had but one ruling passion in life — power and money. Rina stood between him and the realization of his ambition.

Vaile was Lionel's private secretary and manager of the Quest's vast estates. For twenty years he had held the post. A born organizer, he had made himself indispensable to the younger man, who had neither Vaile's brains nor judgment.

During the last years at Foracza, the two men had become more than master and employee. They had been friends, calling each other by their Christian names; riding, shooting, fishing and hunting together. Hannen Vaile held Lionel's complete trust. And then, one day, boar-hunting in the forests surrounding the castle, Hannen had saved Lionel's life.

In a fit of gratitude, Lionel had sworn to make Hannen his heir.

'I shall never marry. You shall inherit my money and my castle,' he had promised. 'I have no next-of-kin.'

Then, in less than a year, to Hannen's bitter rage and disappointment, Lionel announced his forthcoming marriage to the English girl. And Rina came, with her red hair and green, black-lashed eyes, and exquisite figure — a far more powerful influence in Lionel Quest's life than Hannen Vaile could ever hope to be.

Hannen saw now that Rina would probably bear Lionel a son, that his hopes of power in Hungary and of a fortune were sliding from his grasp. Lionel had tried to smooth things over. He had promised his secretary a generous sum of money and certain lands when he retired. But Hannen — a man of unlimited ambition — was dissatisfied. He hankered after his old expectations. He wanted to get Rina out of the way. And he saw no way of doing it, save by poisoning Lionel's mind against her. But to Rina he always appeared suave, polite, charming, as though he were one of her most ardent admirers.

It was obvious to Vaile that he must act quickly if he hoped to stop the marriage. Lionel was impatiently awaiting Rina's recovery. He spoke of little else save his wedding.

Rina was confined to her room, dejected and worried, harassed by the incessant thought of the gypsy whose influence over her was so great.

The day after her collapse she received Lionel in her room and assured him that she was still ill.

'Perhaps tomorrow I shall be better, but today I feel quite awful,' she said.

Indeed, she looked so pale, so delicate, lying in the great bed, that Lionel was ready to believe her. He kissed her hand from finger to wrist.

'Hurry up and get well again, darling,' he said. 'I want my wife.'

'Dear Lionel . . . ' she murmured.

But after he had gone she turned her face to the pillow and her fingers dragged nervously, angrily, at the chain about her throat. She was frightened, desperate. When would Miska come again? What would be his next move? She thought of his lips, hard and demanding against her mouth, and trembled in the thrall of an emotion too chaotic to be definable.

Lionel was attentive and sympathetic. Every day fresh flowers were sent by him up to her bedroom. Each morning, Madame Quest paid her a visit with the doctor. Leaning on her ebony stick, she would sit and gossip a bit and tell Rina how impatient they were for her complete recovery.

At the end of four days, Rina found that she could no longer postpone the marriage. The doctor pronounced her to be well enough to stand the excitement and strain of the wedding. She was forced to get up, to tell Lionel that tomorrow she would marry him. But she was afraid. The chain seemed to eat into her throat under the scarf which she wore around her neck to hide it. It scorched her flesh — like Miska's kisses.

Lionel was delighted at her recovery.

That night he asked Hannen Vaile and his best man, Captain Lipto, to dine with them at the Castle.

Hannen Vaile arrived in excellent form, his black eyes gleaming with excitement. He had just received a wonderful piece of news from one of his agents: news which he relished and kept until the end of the evening.

They were sitting in the big library, the windows open to the night, the sweet mountain air blowing softly upon them. A great white wolf-hound, which Lionel had given to Rina that morning, lay on the rug at her feet.

Rina, in black velvet with Lionel's pearls twisted about her throat, had been trying bravely all evening to be gay and amusing, not to betray her inner feelings of doubt and fear about the ceremony tomorrow.

She looked very lovely. Lionel seldom took his gaze from her. The postponement of his marriage had made him doubly keen. How wonderful her white skin looked against that black velvet, he thought. Captain Lipto was also entranced by her beauty. But Hannen Vaile, unstirred, coldly ambitious, looked at Rina, as much as he would have looked at a snake, with loathing. She came between him and his passion for power. But he had an unpleasant surprise in store for her. He would spring it now, and watch her reactions.

Captain Lipto had just been singing. He was a good musician like most of his countrymen. Lionel had asked him to give Rina a selection of Hungarian folk-songs. Lipto sang well, but every note was a secret torment to Rina. She heard only the haunting voice of the man who had sung on the barge going down the Danube, the man into whose arms she had walked when he had finished his wild passionate song of love — a song such as Lipto was singing now.

Rina sat back in her chair, her hands clenched tightly, trying to keep back the tears which welled in her eyes. Then Hannen Vaile's cool, precise voice fell like ice-water in the room.

'I had interesting news today,' he said, when Captain Lipto sat down.

'What was it, Hannen?' Lionel asked, lighting a cigar.

'It concerns Miska the Gypsy . . . ' Vaile's gaze turned to Rina. She sat still, her eyes shut.

'What about that devil?'

'He is dead . . . '

'*Dead!*' Lionel repeated eagerly. 'You are sure, certain of your facts?'

'Quite. He was found in a ravine in the mountains with a knife through his back,' said Vaile slowly, as though relishing each word.

He kept his eyes on Rina. She had opened hers now and was looking at him, her gaze one of sick horror. She was ghastly white.

He thought:

'She loved him, obviously. Lionel is a fool.'

The three men discussed the notorious gypsy's death. Rina, her heart beating madly, kept silence. Hannen recounted what he knew. It was a report from one of his agents, a man he could trust. While he was talking, Lionel walked to Rina's side.

'You look pale, my dearest. Would you like to leave us — to go to your room?'

She stood up. Her heart ceased its wild, painful hammering now; died down to slow, agonizing beats. She felt like a dead thing. But she smiled towards Lionel and nodded her head.

'I think I will go up,' she said. 'I feel tired.'

Lionel kissed her hand. Captain Litpo clicked his heels together and bowed. Hannen Vaile bowed also, his ironic gaze following the graceful figure as she left the room and began slowly to climb the great staircase to her bedroom.

Once alone in her room, Rina sank on to the bed and put her head between her hands. So this was the end! Miska was dead. Her imagination was only too vivid. She pictured that powerful, graceful body stiff and still; the intense, strangely handsome brown face upturned to the stars; those eagle eyes wide and staring; all the vitality, the hot blood and passion of him, for ever stilled.

She had loved him. Loved him madly and hated him madly. But now it was ended. She would never see him again. There would be no more threats or terrorism; never again would she feel the fierce clasp of his arms, the terrifying, yet thrilling, passion of his kisses.

Tomorrow she could, without fear, take her vows as Lionel's wife.

She thought:

'If there had been peace between us — if he had stayed as the Michael of the barge — I could have loved him for ever.'

But now her heart felt dead within her. She knew that she would never love any man again.

That night seemed interminable to Rina. Sleep was out of the question. She could only pray for the hours to pass more quickly, that the morning would help her to forget.

At last the hot, languorous Hungarian day dawned, and once more Rina found herself being dressed for her wedding. This time nothing prevented the ceremony. Lionel awaited her at the altar rails, even more eager than before. The old priest united them. Rina was made Lionel Quest's wife and mistress of the Castle.

When the ring was slipped on her finger, she closed her eyes, her face pale under the golden veil. She remembered her other marriage in the mountains and Miska's hard brown fingers gripping hers. The chain was still about her throat. Even Miska's death had not unforged those links, nor ever would, she told herself.

Hannen Vaile witnessed the ceremony. His face was a mask of ill-suppressed rage. But the majority of the guests were delighted. The Castle was gay with an atmosphere of festivity, the great rooms crowded with people, full of movement. All afternoon there was music, dancing, feasting. Lionel was enchanted with his bride; and she, exquisitely beautiful, received his friends and their guests with a smile on her red lips, an incessant smile which hid her desire to weep — to weep wild, bitter tears over the mountain-grave of her first, her only, lover.

When night came with its jewelled sky and new sickle moon, the Castle windows glittered with a thousand lights; the floodlit, flower-filled gardens were a picture of beauty. Bride and groom received more guests who arrived for the ball, which was to be the culmination of the wedding celebrations. The officers of the guard were present, their splendid uniforms eclipsing even the lovely, colourful gowns of the women. In the musicians' gallery of the great hall a Viennese orchestra played softly.

Rina, her face flushed by the champagne which she had deliberately taken in order to keep up her spirits, danced tirelessly all evening. With Lionel an old-fashioned waltz. With Captain Lipto a fox-trot. And a Hungarian dance with the Colonel of the Guard. They told her how beautiful she looked in her ball-dress. It was old ivory lace, sewn with sequins. Lionel's diamonds were flashing about her throat, and there was a ruby and diamond tiara on her head. She knew that she looked like a queen; that she eclipsed every other woman in the room. But she was weary and sick at heart. Whenever Lionel threw her an adoring look, or touched her hand, she had to force herself to smile back at him.

Later that evening she wandered from the crowd and stood, a glass of champagne in her hand, gazing out of the window at the stars. The glamour of the night passed her by. She realized that she had drunk too much wine. Her head ached unbearably. If she did not get some fresh air she felt she could not carry on. She knew that she must make an effort to gain some semblance of control before she returned to Lionel's guests.

Taking a cigarette from a thin gold case in her bag, she lit it and turned towards the ballroom. Then she heard footsteps behind her and a man's deep voice.

'May I claim this waltz, Madame?'

She looked slowly round. She faced a tall man in the white-and-gold uniform of the Hungarian guards. He wore a small military cape and gold epaulettes. A handsome man with black, curly hair and a well-trimmed beard. He bowed low over her hand.

Rina put a hand to her eyes. Her pulses jerked unevenly. Her head was reeling. Where had she seen this man before? Nowhere. But of whom did he remind her? Of Miska? Yes, of Miska. He had the same thick, raven-dark hair, the same hard brown face.

Without speaking, scarcely knowing what she did, Rina moved towards him. He put an arm lightly about her. A moment later they were waltzing in the midst of the brilliant throng.

When she was in his arms, Rina's body stiffened. She stared up at him, wide-eyed, her heart pounding wildly.

'I must be mad,' she told herself, 'or drunk! Miska is dead.'

Then, closing her eyes, she gave herself up to the dance. The bearded stranger danced magnificently. Her head still reeled alarmingly and she leaned against him. He looked down at her, at the black lashes which lay like small silken fans against the soft pink of her cheeks.

When she opened her eyes again she found that she was waltzing with the stranger on the moon-flooded terrace. He had guided her out of the ballroom. The lilting Hungarian music grew fainter. Her partner let go her hand, but kept an arm still about her. He led her down the marble stairs past the window of Hannen Vaile's room, where, unknown to them both, Lionel's secretary watched, a sardonic smile on his lips.

In the garden, the moon shed an earthly radiance upon the shadowy lawn. Rina, in that brilliant light, looked like an exquisite silver statue. But it was a statue that came to life, like Galatea in the arms of her creator.

For Rina found herself in *Miska's* arms, his voice, *Miska's voice*, was close to her ears.

'You are right, beloved,' he whispered. 'It is Miska — your lover. Don't try to think — to understand. Forget everything — but this.'

She was caught and held madly against his breast. His lips were upon hers, fiercely, possessively. His sensitive brown fingers caught the chain about her neck and kissed it.

'Mine, mine,' he whispered between each kiss.

Rina lay panting in his arms. Her heart seemed to burst within her. *So he was not dead!* Or was it the wine intoxicating her? Was she dreaming? Truth or delusion, whatever it was, she drowned now in a veritable whirlpool of passion. His kisses burned her throat, her arms, her lips. Half-consciously she yielded her whole body to that wild embrace.

Then suddenly the peace of the moonlit garden was broken by the hoarse shouting of men, of running footsteps and flickering lanterns.

Miska lifted his head sharply. He went pale under his bronze. He released Rina, but before he could move he was surrounded by a dozen uniformed men. Amongst them was Lionel, and Hannen Vaile, a cold, triumphant smile on his face.

Captain Lipto, who last night had sung folk-songs for Rina, put a hand on Miska's shoulder.

'I arrest you in the name of the law,' he said in a cold silky, satisfied voice.

Rina looked round her with dilated eyes. Then Miska's eagle glance caught hers and held it. She heard his low, bitter voice.

'Not loyal in love. Not loyal in anything in this world. You knew who I was, knew when you danced with me. You brought me here to give me to your husband's guards. You took my kisses — in order to give the men time to come after me . . . '

He made a sudden movement towards her, shaking with rage and bitterness. Two guards gripped his arm and drew him back.

'Take him and lock him up,' said Lionel's harsh voice.

Then something in Rina seemed to break. Miska had denounced her before these people. He called her a traitoress, believed that she was disloyal. Very well. She could show him that she was not going to be bullied, dominated by him any longer.

'You are right,' she cried hysterically, two scarlet spots on her white cheeks. 'Quite right. I *did* know who you were — you fool! I'm glad, *glad* they've got you . . . ' She choked and clenched her small jewelled hands. 'Glad they will lock you up, where you belong.'

Miska's eyes, brilliant with fury and

scorn, glared at her. Then, holding up a shaking hand, he cursed her in the Magyar language — a gypsy malediction.

'Never more may you know peace or contentment in any lover's arms. Never will you laugh with love's laughter, nor weep with love's happy tears, nor thrill to the lips of passion. Never, save in my arms, will you know one instant's pleasure, and if I die, a withered, unsatisfied, unfulfilled destiny shall be yours!'

The superstitious Hungarian soldiers fell back, shuddering at the love-curse of the Magyars.

Lionel uttered an oath.

'Take this maniac away,' he ordered furiously.

Miska laughed as he was hurried off by the guards. The laughter was the last thing Rina heard before she fell, fainting, into Lionel's arms.

She was carried to her suite in the Castle, a white, still figure with closed eyes and piteous mouth.

She knew nothing until she found herself lying on her bed, undressed, her two maids anxiously fanning her face and bathing her temples with eau-de-Cologne.

Once realization came back to her she lay like one dead, staring up at the ceiling with wide frightened eyes, little shudders passing through her body.

She remembered the moment of revelation, when she had found herself with Miska, her gypsy lover, and how she had yielded to his fierce, passionate embrace. What then? Lionel's coming, and Miska's arrest.

Where was he? What were they going to do about the whole affair?

Panic-stricken, she told herself that she was not Lionel's wife. She had had no right to marry him in the chapel this morning. She had been made Miska's wife by gypsy-law, in the mountains. *His* bride she was! She asked herself if she would have ever taken those vows to Lionel this morning, had she not been labouring under the delusion that

Miska was dead.

She had grieved for him. Her heart had ached and bled at the thought of his tragic death. But now that she knew that he lived, what did she feel? She hardly knew. Her emotions were too confused. But she was fully aware of the fact that he despised her, that he had cursed her — and her whole spirit rebelled against it.

She must see Lionel, find out what was going to happen to Miska. Ringing the bell by her bed, she summoned one of her maids.

'Ask His Excellency to come here — at once,' she ordered.

Lionel came to her bedside in a mood which was quite foreign to her. He was livid with fury and resentment. He stood glaring down at her, his fairish skin flushed red, his mouth ugly.

'I'm sorry, Lionel,' Rina faltered, holding out a hand.

'Sorry!' he echoed. 'God knows, you ought to be! It is incredible that I, Lionel Quest, should find my wife in the arms of that damned gypsy — that brigand notorious for his crimes against the laws of Hungary . . . that brown-skinned Magyar . . . ' He stopped, choking with temper.

Rina looked at him anxiously. She saw that jealousy, primitive and thwarted passion, had completely transformed the man whom she had always known to be cold and quietly reticent.

'Let me try to explain, Lionel,' she said. 'The man had been drinking. He couldn't stop talking. When we were dancing, he boasted that he was Miska, that you could not catch him. He didn't know what he was saying, it was the wine talking. I tried to get him into the garden in order to attract the soldiers . . . '

'Was it necessary to kiss him in order to keep him there?' Lionel sneered.

Rina felt the colour flood her cheeks.

'Don't be a fool, Lionel,' she said. 'I didn't kiss him. I tell you the man was drunk, he didn't know what he was doing. But I played up to it all, knowing that if I kept him long enough, you would come.'

Lionel looked down at her with doubt. Hannen Vaile had poisoned his mind against the girl. Yet perhaps he had misjudged her. Perhaps it was true that she had submitted to the man's kisses in order to trap him. Lionel *wanted* to think so. He took her outstretched fingers.

'You swear that is true, Rina?'

She felt that she was, in some mysterious way, betraying all that was best in her when she answered:

'I swear it!'

Lionel swung from doubt to relief. Sinking on one knee beside her bed, he kissed her hand.

'I've been crazy with jealousy, Rina — ever since I saw you in that man's arms, I've been half mad. I love you. You are my wife.'

She closed her eyes and breathed fast.

'Be patient, Lionel. The whole thing has been a shock, a strain.'

At once he rose and moved away from her.

'Forgive me, my darling. I'll send your maid to you. Of course you have been upset. Any girl would be. It was a foul experience for you. Tomorrow I will stay with you — my lovely wife!'

He left the room, once more believing in her and in her love. She lay like a broken flower, a bird captured, netted, tangled up — wondering which way to escape from the net. She had not even dared to ask him what he meant to do with Miska. She felt panic-stricken and helpless.

Lionel went to his study, confident that she had told him the truth. He was more than ever her slave, certain that tomorrow he would have her in his arms — his bride. He was willing to stamp on his jealousy, to laugh at Hannen's suspicions.

He told his secretary so as he passed him in one of the long corridors.

'I have just been speaking to my wife, Hannen,' he said curtly. 'I am satisfied with her explanation about tonight's incident. I don't want it mentioned again.'

Hannen Vaile did not reply. It made him furious to think that once again Lionel was at Rina's feet. The man was a fool! He, Hannen Vaile, had shown Lionel his wife in the gypsy's arms. Was that not enough? The fellow must be mad to be so coerced by that red-haired, green-eyed slip of a girl. Mad to credit her version of the story.

Miska the Gypsy was in a cell under the Castle, safely under lock and key. But that was not going to benefit Vaile. He did not really care what happened to Miska. All he wanted, and he wanted it desperately, was to get Lionel away from Rina, to prevent any possibility of the birth of a son and heir to Lionel.

5

One o'clock in the morning found Vaile still dressed, pacing his rooms, brooding over the affair. At the end of his thinking and worrying he decided that there was only one hope left. He must effect Miska's escape. It would be a masterly move if he could be certain that the gypsy would take Rina with him. There seemed little doubt that he wanted her. He had risked his life coming to the Castle to see her. When he had cursed her publicly, tonight, he had suggested to the world that he was her lover.

Vaile opened the door of his room and looked out. The corridor was dark and silent. Carrying a lamp in his hand, he hurried through the Castle towards the stone spiral staircase which led down to the dungeons.

It was chilly and dark, malodorous

with damp. A rat scuttled away at the approach of a man. The luxury-loving secretary shivered and drew his coat about his shoulders. This was a foul spot.

He found a guard posted outside Miska's cell. The man saluted Vaile. In the Castle, orders came from Hannen Vaile more often than from his master. The guard was not surprised when the secretary told him that he could go off duty.

'I wish to interview the prisoner,' said Hannen Vaile. 'You can take a few hour's sleep.'

The man went off gladly. It was depressing work, standing about in this cold, dark prison under the Castle. A moment later Vaile unlocked the cell and entered, carrying the lamp with him.

Miska had been lying on a straw pallet, sleepless, grim and bitterly cold. He sprang up when the door opened. He had had three very unpleasant hours in the cell. The rats disturbed him, and the close, sour atmosphere filled him with depression, used as he was to sleeping in the fresh mountain air under the stars.

He had taken off the false beard which he had been forced to wear that night. The thing annoyed him. It savoured of cheap, childish deceit. The light from Vaile's lamp fell on his face and dazzled him. There was silence for a moment, and then he heard a muffled oath.

'Michael Quest! *You!*' Vaile cried. His voice had lost all trace of its usual calm. 'God in heaven, you are not the gypsy! You are Michael Quest!'

The younger man shrugged his shoulder.

'I am Miska,' he said, stressing the name.

'Then Miska and Michael Quest are one and the same!'

'You say so. I do not. Why have *you* come to see me?'

Hannen Vaile did not answer. Setting the lamp on a bracket, he stared as though unable to believe his eyes at the man who, arms crossed over his chest, returned his scrutiny with some defiance on his tired, grim young face.

A host of memories returned to Hannen Vaile. He went back twenty years ago, to the time when he had first come to the Castle as Lionel's secretary. Then, there had been another Quest in the Castle. Michael, Lionel's brother and junior by a year. Michael — brown-browed, passionate, impulsive, like his wild Hungarian ancestors, who had always been the antithesis of the cold, prosaic Lionel.

Hannen had never liked the boy. He knew that Michael saw through him. Michael had realized with a clarity of vision beyond his years that Hannen was out for what he could get for himself; that he was more than a worker for his master's interest.

Michael had always been the favourite with their tutor and with the servants in the Castle. They loved him for his frank, spontaneous manner. But

Madame Quest, cold and severe, liked her eldest son, preferred Lionel. She misunderstood the passionate, impulsive temperament of her younger boy.

Michael was always in trouble. Hannen knew that Lionel hated his brother secretly, and in an underhand malicious fashion helped to poison his mother against him and magnify Michael's youthful follies into vicious sins.

The situation had remained the same until the day when a young Hungarian maid, a pretty child of seventeen in Madame Quest's employ, had been found drowned in one of the lakes in the Castle grounds. It was a sordid affair, a plain case of suicide. The girl had left a note for her mother asking for her forgiveness, in which she also declared that the cruelty and desertion of the Herr Quest, who had been her lover, had driven her to take her life.

Blame fell at once on Michael. But Michael was innocent. It was Lionel who had carried on an intrigue with a sentimental child. He knew it. Hannen Vale knew it. Michael knew it, but nobody else. And when Lionel — a coward at heart — thrust the blame on his brother, everybody believed that the handsome, wild, gypsy-hearted Michael was the culprit.

The blame was more than Michael's sensitive mind could stand. He decided to leave the Castle and his family for ever. Furious, embittered, wounded by the injustice of his brother and his enemies, he ran away. His name was never again mentioned in the family. Rina had not even been told that Lionel had a brother.

Hannen Vaile was more than shocked to find him here, to discover that Miska, the notorious Magyar of the mountains, was Michael Quest, and to discover what the years had made of him.

If Vaile had dreaded Lionel's marriage and the possibility of him having a son, still more did he dread the return of Michael, who was at the moment

Lionel's legal successor. Hannen had believed that the wild boy was dead. Well, now it was more than ever important that he should get both Michael and Rina away.

He narrowed his gaze and spoke softly.

'You intend to keep the name of Miska the Gypsy?'

'I do,' said Michael tersely.

'You have no inclination to return here?'

'None, thanks.' The younger man's voice was bitter.

Vaile nodded.

'And what of your brother's bride?'

Michael stiffened and clenched his hands.

'What about her?'

'You want her?'

'I have cursed her,' he answered. 'I despise her. I want her only because she belongs to me.'

Vaile smiled.

'That will suit me, my young friend. I am not friends with the red-haired Rina.'

Michael maintained a contemptuous silence. He knew Vaile of old, knew his expectations. But he did not care. He hated this Castle and every memory of his unhappy, misjudged boyhood. Vaile said:

'I will give you your freedom, Michael. On one condition.'

'Which is . . . ?'

'That you take Rina with you.'

Michael smiled, a slow smile, but there was a red blaze behind his handsome eyes.

'Give me the chance, Hannen Vaile.'

'You shall have it — within a few hours. I shall send her to you with a skeleton key. Meanwhile, I will give this key to your guard and tell him to return to duty at dawn. Just before dawn you will get away. I will see that you are not stopped at the gates.'

A shade of ironic humour curved Michael's lips.

'Your kindness overwhelms me, Hannen,' he said. 'You were not always so friendly.'

Vaile shrugged his shoulders.

'I prefer that you and the red-haired witch are out of this.'

'I prefer to be out of it,' Michael answered.

'Very well. Now remember what I've told you. Just before dawn. And you'd better take this,' he said, taking a small bottle from his pocket. 'It is ether. Your lovely Rina may not be so keen to go away with you. Now good night. We may not meet again.'

'Not if I can help it!'

Hannen Vaile smiled his slow, cold smile and departed.

Michael sat down on the straw pallet in the chill, dark cell. His heart was beating fast. His eyes gleamed. He would be free again in a few hours — and Rina would go with him. He clenched his hands. Yes, he would take her. She was all his. He would punish her for what she had done to him tonight.

'*Red-haired witch!*' Vaile had called her. The man was right. She *was* a witch, with her fatal beauty and appeal.

But he, Miska, was not going to succumb to that witchery. He knew her to be light and disloyal. The next time she was in his arms she would not respond so sweetly to his kisses. She would beg for respite from them. He felt that he could kill her — kill her with his fierce love and scorn, and feel her heart throb with terror under his passionate hand.

Miska the Gypsy lay down and waited. Sleepless, expectant, strangely triumphant, he waited for the moment of his liberation.

Half an hour before the grey dawn broke over the Castle, Rina awoke to feel a light touch on her hand. She sat up, startled, wide awake. She had just fallen into a heavy sleep of sheer fatigue. No light burned in the luxurious bedroom. The curtains were still drawn. The door was closed. Someone had come in, touched her and vanished again.

For a moment she thought that it must have been Lionel, then she saw that an envelope was lying on her pillow. When she ripped it open, a key fell out. With wide, scared eyes she read the words written in print on a sheet of paper.

Miska is to be shot at dawn. If you wish to say farewell, take this key and go down to the dungeon. Be cautious. Tell nobody.

There was no signature. Only those significant words and the key. Rina, her face ashen, stared round the room. Michael — to be shot at dawn! Oh God, it couldn't be true! Michael, with his marvellous vitality and love of life — to be shot in cold blood. And he thinking that *she* had betrayed him, that she had *wished* it to happen.

'I must see him,' she thought feverishly. 'I must tell him, make him understand that it wasn't my fault. I must tell him that before he dies. But he must not die! He can't!'

Blindly flinging on some clothes, she

took an electric torch from her dressing-table and, shivering with nerves and cold, crept out of her room, the key clenched in her hand.

She knew the way. One afternoon, when she had been walking through the Castle with Lionel, he had jokingly pointed out the circular staircase which led down to the subterranean passages.

'That's where I shall send you if you're a bad wife,' he had laughed.

The steps were steep and slippery with damp. She walked carefully on her high-heeled little shoes. She flashed the torch only when it was needed. She kept thinking:

'I *must* tell him. He must believe me. They can't shoot him. I won't let them. If they do, they shall shoot me, too.'

With a shaking hand she unlocked the heavy wooden door of the cell. It creaked loudly on its hinges. Then there was silence.

'Michael,' she whispered. 'It is Rina. Michael, speak to me! Tell me it isn't true.'

She flashed on her torch and held it aloft. Michael was standing at the far end of the cell, his face grim, forbidding. He gave a short laugh.

'So you have come, my loyal wife!'

'Michael — you don't understand,' she began frantically.

'I understand only one thing,' he broke in. 'You lured me into a trap — betrayed me — and I despise you.'

'I've come to tell you that isn't true.'

'There is no time for your lies — or for arguments,' he said roughly. 'I'm going to get out of this hole and you are going with me.'

'What do you mean?'

Michael did not reply. Suddenly he moved towards her. The torch went out, plunging the cell into darkness. Rina gave a cry. Then she felt Michael's arms about her. For an instant she felt his lips brush hers.

'You are going with me now,' he said. 'From now on you will do as *I* wish.'

'No, Michael — '

The words died in her throat. A pad

was thrust against her nostrils. A sweet, sickly smell filled the cell. Choking and coughing, Rina gave a little moan. The fumes of the ether robbed her of power of speech and action.

She did not remember the moment when she ceased to struggle. She knew nothing of being picked up in Michael's arms and carried out of the cell along the passages. Passages of which Michael knew every inch, where as a boy he had played hide-and-seek.

She knew nothing until, conscious of a sense of nausea, she opened her eyes, to find herself back in the warm, gaily coloured cave of Miska the Gypsy. Then she knew that, once more, she was a captive in his gypsy kingdom in the mountains, seven thousand feet above Foracza.

It was a bitter awakening for her.

Miska sat at a table, smoking, once more in his Magyar clothes. The door of the cave was half open. Sunlight streamed through, and fresh mountain air blew softly upon her.

The man looked tired and thoughtful. He had been sitting there a long time, smoking his cigarettes, watching Rina, thinking in bitterness of soul how lovely she looked with her glorious red head against his cushions, her pale face framed in the silver-fox collar of her coat, like the face of a slumbering, lovely child. Lovely and treacherous. From the very beginning on the barge, coming down the Danube, she had tricked him, he thought. Now she must pay.

Rina sat up, her heavy lashes lifting, her wide green eyes searching the cave.

'So you have brought me back!'

He nodded.

'Yes. And this time you stay!'

She rose unsteadily to her feet. She felt sick and wretched. Her head ached unbearably. But she faced him courageously.

'You make one great mistake,' she said. 'I will not stay — *at your command.*'

Jumping to his feet, he made one

swift movement towards her and drew her into the circle of his arm.

'I think you will,' he said. 'You are mine.' His fingers touched the chain about her neck. 'That binds us. Even though I despise you, Rina, that chain makes you mine. At least I can keep you to amuse me!'

'You won't find me very amusing,' she said, her eyes burning with anger.

'That is for me to say.' He kissed her lips and her throat, threading his fingers through her hair. 'Come, my darling! You look tragic. Let my kisses make up for Lionel's!'

Rina was powerless. She wanted to hurt him, to get away from his arms. But it was hopeless. He held her more tightly, laughing softly to himself. His lips strayed from her mouth to her eyes, her cheeks, her hair.

'Damn you!' she cried. 'I wish they *had* shot you . . . '

'My sweet!' he laughed. 'Why so shy? It isn't the first time that I have held you in my arms, that you have felt my heart beat so wildly for love of you. Kiss me — as you kissed me in the garden last night — before you were deprived of the sadistic pleasure of seeing me shot!'

'You fool,' she said. 'Mad fool — let me go!'

He shrugged his shoulders.

'Very well,' he said releasing her from his arms. 'We shall have plenty of time together. It's too late now to turn your back on my love. You can't just lock your heart at will and take away the key from me.'

Rina flung herself on the couch, her face hidden in her hands, her body shaking. She realized that she need expect no mercy. The man who had fascinated her so wildly meant to exert his ownership only out of revenge — not love. And she told herself that she hated him for it with all her heart and soul.

Turning his back on her, Michael moved out of the cave into the sunlight. He thought he had heard the murmur

137

of voices through the open door. Now he saw that a crowd of gypsies was hanging about outside. Zsil, his trusted leader, stood at the head of them. Michael was surprised. Zsil looked sullen and angry. There was a general atmosphere of dissatisfaction which Michael did not understand.

'What is it, Zsil?' he asked curtly.

Zsil put a hand on his hip and regarded his master menacingly. He was a swarthy, tight-lipped man. A livid triangular scar running down one side of his face accentuated his already sinister appearance. Michael had always regarded him as his most trusted servant. He had made him head man, instructed him, taught him to speak English.

There had been no opportunity for Michael to discover that Zsil was innately unscrupulous and grasping, that he had served him only with one end — to take Miska's place, finally, at the head of the tribe. Michael knew nothing of this evil which had been brewing in Zsil's heart.

'What is it?' Michael repeated sharply, lifting his handsome head with a proud gesture.

Rina, in the cave, raised herself from the couch where she had been lying and walked to the door. Her heart beat fearfully, her tear-swollen eyes searched the crowd. How sullen, how menacing they all looked! What was happening? She wished that she could understand the language Zsil was speaking.

Michael understood — only too well. As he listened, his face grew grim, his eyes steely.

'Perhaps you do not know, Miska,' Zsil was saying in a harsh, disrespectful voice, 'that the Englishman at the Castle is offering a huge reward of gold, both for the return of the girl and for your life. Your capture of this girl has raised a hornets' nest about our ears.'

'There was no question of this the other night,' Michael replied evenly. 'The tribe was pleased. The people rejoiced at my wedding.'

'That was different,' Zsil replied angrily. 'We thought you would keep her here, in the safety of our caves. We did not expect you to return her. We did not expect you to visit the Castle; visits which can only end in disaster for us all.'

Michael looked into the man's menacing eyes.

'My visits to the Castle are finished. The girl stays here now . . . '

'It is too late,' Zsil told him. 'The people say it is too dangerous and they say she must go. You can hear what they want.' He turned and called to the crowd outside the cave. 'Tell Miska what you wish.'

'Zsil is right,' the crowd shouted. 'Give us the woman, Miska!'

'Hear you!' said Zsil, turning to Michael, one hand on the hilt of the dagger in his scarlet belt. 'The people demand the girl.'

'Are you insane?' Michael asked.

The tribe surged closer, muttering, casting threatening glances towards

Rina who, pale and terrified, stood behind Michael.

'Give us the girl that we may return her to Foracza,' said Zsil. 'Do this and once more you may be king amongst us.'

Michael's grey eyes blazed.

'Am I king no longer, then?' he said between set teeth, and he too put a hand on his knife.

A thousand blades glittered in the sunshine. The gypsies raised their weapons at Miska. Miska, whom they had adored, whom they would willingly have followed to the death, was an alien in their sight. Their childish, fickle fancy swayed to Zsil, their blood-brother.

'Give her to us,' repeated Zsil harshly. 'If you do not, then surely you will die!'

Rina caught at Michael's arm.

'What is it, Michael? What do they say?'

He turned to her.

'They say that unless I send you back to Lionel, they will kill me.'

She clutched his hand.

'Then let me go, Michael. Let me go now before it's too late. For God's sake, Michael. They will kill you. Let me go.'

'Like hell I will!'

Rina did not try to understand. He had said that he loathed and despised her. Surely, then, to save his life he would give her up to them? But if he did, would they really return her to Lionel, or would they keep her for themselves? The people were wild, undisciplined. She had seen Zsil and another man beside him looking at her, not with the light of revenge in their black, cruel eyes — but with a blaze of passion.

She looked up into Michael's eyes. It was obvious that he was neither cowed nor terrorized by the murmurings and the lifted knives. The disloyalty and childish jealousy of the whole affair had angered him to the pitch of madness. His tall body trembled. His brown, handsome face was livid as he glared round him.

'Listen, all of you!' he cried furiously. 'I am Miska — and your king. Many years ago you took me as your leader. You, Zsil,' he narrowed his gaze menacingly towards the gypsy, whose sinister face reddened, 'I trusted. *You* wish to betray me. I would like to kill you like the wolf that you are. But I will not soil my weapon with your blood. I do not fear your puny threats. There is not one amongst you who dare put me to death. For he who kills the man who is acknowledged to be king will surely be cursed to the end of his days. This woman is mine. None shall take her from me. Now go back to your caves and let there be peace!'

Michael held up his hand for silence. He looked down at Rina. The sunlight had caught and turned her hair to splendid red. Suddenly he moved towards her, and taking her in his arms, kissed her lips in full sight of the people. Then, taking her hand, he led her towards the cave.

Zsil snarled at the crowd of gypsies around him.

'Fools,' he sneered. 'Will you let him intimidate you?'

The men began to argue amongst themselves. Zsil shouted at them, inciting them to fresh rebellion.

'We do not wish to be cursed,' called one of the older men.

Zsil turned to him.

'You will be cursed by this girl,' he said. 'She is a witch. She has put a spell on Miska. He must either give her to us — or die.'

'Agreed,' came from a hundred throats.

They remained, surging about Zsil, arguing, protesting. The majority appeared to be on the side of the rebel. The women folk, who had adored Miska for his physical beauty and courage, whispered amongst themselves. They dared not speak.

Inside the cave Rina watched Michael breathlessly. He was tying a quantity of food and bread in a scarlet handkerchief, filling his leather belt with cartridges, making a bundle of rugs and shawls.

'What are you doing?' she asked, a hand to her throat.

He looked at her, his sensitive lips set in a thin line.

'I'm not giving you up, Rina . . . '

'Then they will kill you.'

'Let them get me first!' he said between his teeth. 'The treacherous dogs! If I had only myself to think about, I would stay and face them out. But I want you and I don't intend to risk *your* neck.'

'You could never get away . . . '

'You shall see!' Taking her hand, he led her to the far end of the cave, and, pushing aside a Persian rug which hung from the roof, revealed a door of solid rock. 'This leads to the other side of the ridge,' he whispered. 'We'll make a dash for it.'

His defiance of the tribe, his courageous independence, filled Rina with a burning admiration which she could not deny. She gave him a swift warm look. His eyes answered hers. For an instant he caught and held her close.

'Do you wish to come with me, or shall I leave you and let you go back to Lionel?'

Rina knew that she would go. Her sense of bitterness and hatred was forgotten. She realized, once more, that this man had only to call and she must answer, must follow him to the world's end. If he were escaping from his enemies into exile, then she would fly with him. For a single breathless moment she clung to him. A wave of emotion swept over them both — engulfing, drowning them.

'Take me,' she said, in a scarcely audible voice.

Michael's face was transfigured. His eyes gleamed. Holding her hand tightly, he led her out towards the sunshine.

Rina saw a vast panorama of space above and below her. Blue sky, sunshine like molten gold sweeping down the green mountain side, an undulating line of shadowy blue mountains to the right and left. Below, like black dots, the shadow of forests, the village of Foracza and the Quests' Castle.

A magnificent mare with a satin chestnut coat was tethered near the exit of the cave. Michael flung a saddle on its back and fixed the bridle and reins. Then jumping into the saddle he helped Rina to mount behind him. She held him round the waist. His right hand gripped the reins and he touched the horse lightly with his heel.

'Away,' he called. 'Upwards, my lovely . . . '

The animal leaped forward into the sunshine. Rina, clinging to Michael, looked over her shoulder. There was not a soul to be seen, no sign of life behind the encampment.

Not until they were out of sight of the caves did Michael turn the mare's head leftwards. Then they started to climb up the mountain side. The animal picked its way surely, delicately, through the rough grass and bracken until they reached the summit from where, it seemed to Rina, she could see the whole world.

'There is a forest on the side of this mountain,' Michael told her. 'We will camp there tonight. Tomorrow we can go on towards the Austrian border.'

Rina did not speak. She felt breathless, her heart pounded as she leaned against his body. He was strong and splendid, this lover of hers. A magnificent man for a woman to love and follow. She knew that she loved him more than life itself. The world was well lost for him, convention and civilization were blotted out for her in a wave of primitive adoration.

The horse went steadily on in the radiant sunshine towards the vast Hungarian mountains where the air was keen and sweet, like a benediction upon them. Rina felt she could ride on like this for ever. She pressed her cheek against Michael's shoulder and gave a little sigh.

He looked down at her. She was so fair, so beautiful and desirable — so warm and exciting — riding with him through the solitary mountains. He no longer despised her nor cared what she had done. He, too, was filled with the exultation which enveloped her. She was his woman and she was going into exile with him, driven away at the point of the dagger, flying with him from death.

He loved and desired her, and he admired her courage. He was surprised, too, that she had come so willingly, without dissent. She was once more his lady of the barge, yielding, quiescent and infinitely adorable. He bent to touch her heavy lashes with his lips.

'Rina. You realize what you have done?'

'Yes.'

'You have burned your boats, crossed the Rubicon. You have chosen me against the world. We are going to be exiled together — perhaps for ever.'

'I am glad,' she said.

'I don't understand,' he said simply, 'but it doesn't seem to matter. Nothing matters, except that we are alone together. But why should you come? Why should you want to stay with me?'

'Because I love you.'

Michael reined in the horse and kissed her lips, her hair, her throat. And she, cupping his warm brown face in her hands, returned his kiss.

'My Rina,' he whispered. 'My own lovely Rina.'

'Michael — Miska — whoever you are, whatever you are, I love you. But we must ride on in case they follow.'

'They won't find us,' he laughed gaily. 'I've come a difficult and intricate way.'

'They are so cruel. I'm afraid.'

'You don't need to be,' he said. 'They will not see Miska again.'

He urged on the horse, but he would have liked to rest awhile, holding her to his heart. He was insatiable for her kisses. This new, sweet, strange bond which was being forged between them seemed the most wonderful thing that had ever happened in his world. He ceased to think about the past, to doubt her, to weigh up what had been.

And Rina, her heart singing within her, thought:

'I love him. He is my lover and my husband. I am married to him. Lionel is forgotten. This is a new life. I am born again . . . for Michael . . . '

It was early evening when they reached the forest on the mountain side. They were now, so it seemed to Rina, countless miles from the gypsy encampment, and still farther from Foracza.

They stopped, when Michael directed, for food and rest. Rina thought it must be the most beautiful spot which nature had to offer.

They had left behind the terrific heights which they had ascended from the other side, left the mighty open spaces, the rocky nests of the eagle, the home of the chamois. They came down a gentle slope to the wonders of the forest — virgin forest — the green gloom of trees. The trees were straight and tall with mighty trunks and twisted branches covered with thick foliage which shut out the sunlight. It was cool and quiet save for the music of a brook rippling, crystal-clear through the dimness, and the call, high up in the branches of a Hungarian bird which Rina had never heard before.

In this remote spot, the lovers made their resting-place. Michael, clever with his hands, tore down branches and made a rough hut of green boughs. He spread the rugs which they had bought over the mossy ground — ground which was dry and sweet to smell.

'It's not much of a place to offer my princess,' he said, when he had finished his work and shown it to Rina.

She, her face flushed, her green eyes shining, said:

'It is wonderful. This forest is the most beautiful place I have ever seen.'

'I'm glad, dearest,' he said.

'There is a divine peace here, Michael,' she told him. 'It is a world of its own — a simple, primeval world with no ugliness, no cruelty, no restriction. It is perfect.'

'For lovers, a paradise,' he said.

He was strong and brown and tall and bright-eyed, leaning against the mighty tree beneath which they had built their shelter. Picturesque and attractive in his vivid-coloured gypsy costume, his black curly hair ruffled like a boy's. Rina contrasted him with the conventional Lionel. Lionel in his dinner-jacket, with his soft, manicured hands, his haughty, narrow-minded outlook. This Michael was a man to love greatly. Her whole being was transfused with love for him. She held out a hand and said:

'My dear, you do not know how glad I am to have come here with you. My only fear is that they may find us.'

'You need not worry about the next few hours,' he said. 'The future is on the knees of the gods. But this night in our enchanted forest belongs to us.' He took her in his arms and stroked her hair. 'Flame colour. Colour of my heart's blood.'

Night came quickly, and the stars twinkling through the leaves, a bright shaft of moonlight piercing the thick green gloom of the forest, was their only light.

Rina bathed her face and hands in the pure, cool water of the stream. Then she lay down on the mossy bed. The bed which her lover had made for her with his own hands.

Michael was standing near her. She could just see his long, fine face in the spiritual gloom. He was smoking a last cigarette. Then she heard him singing. Singing as he had done on the barge, in his rich stirring voice. Rina raised herself on an elbow and listened. It was a Magyar love-song. A song which throbbed with passion and desire. It was the song which he had sung to her on the Danube. She remembered the wild, heart-stirring words which he had translated for her:

You are the heart of me now.
The breath that I draw.
The wild, passionate breath of my
body.
Keep close to me, beloved.
For if you go, you take from me my
heart . . .

Rina lay still under her rug, her heart and body filled with ecstasy. Stretching her arms above her head, she closed her eyes, which were heavy with love and sleep.

'He is mine and I am his — and I love him,' she thought, tears of wild happiness stinging her eyes.

The Hungarian love-song ceased. Michael came to her, under the green tent of sweet, dry boughs. She felt his hands, warm, possessive, upon her hair; the beat of his heart against hers. He caught and held the gypsy chain about her throat.

'My love,' he whispered. 'You are mine — the heart of me now!'

'I am yours and I love you,' she said brokenly.

'Why are you crying? Your eyes are wet.'

'Only with happiness,' she told him, with a smile which he could not see.

'My Rina. Here in this forest under these stars, I take again every gypsy vow which I made to love and protect you.'

Rina turned towards him. His lips closed upon hers, feverishly, claiming them in endless kisses.

There was silence in the forest save for the unceasing ripple of the brook, the occasional sound of a stray animal in the forest.

Rina, locked in Michael's arms, answered his kisses, his every desire. This was her real wedding-night. She wanted to make it perfect for him, ecstatic, unforgettable. He was her husband. She must raise him to the very heights of rapturous happiness this night.

'Keep close to me, beloved,' she whispered. 'I am yours. I am your woman — 'the wild passionate breath of your body'. You are my husband

— and my lover!'

He drew her to him in the darkness of their shelter, and she knew that this man must always be her lover. She gave him her heart, her warm white body, her soul. She would always want to give. He must always want to take. She could not live without him — without that strong, demanding body which now was part of hers.

6

Rina awoke and stretched her white arms drowsily. A new, golden day had commenced. The forest was filled with the busy song of waking birds. She felt fit and hungry.

Where was Michael?

She left the tent of boughs, her face flushed with the remembrance of last night, her eyes like jewels. How happy she was; how perfectly happy! Walking to the back of the tent, she looked for him. Then she called his name:

'Michael!'

There was no reply. She sat down under a tree to wait, then, glancing up, saw that a note was pinned to the trunk. A few words were scrawled in pencil:

I have gone with my gun to find some food. Light a fire if you can, sweetheart. I love you!

Rina smiled. Her pulses thrilled.

'I love you too, Michael,' she whispered.

She heard a rustle in the trees behind her. Michael was returning! She turned with a smile of welcome, but the smile faded from her face. It was not Michael. It was a strange gypsy, one of the brown fierce-faced men of Miska's tribe.

Her heart seemed to die within her. Had they followed, and routed Michael out? Was this to be the end of their new-found happiness and faith in each other?

The gypsy spoke in halting English.

'Lady, I am Czico. Perhaps you know — most faithful servant to Miska.'

She looked at him taut, wide-eyed, suspicious.

'Is there a faithful servant left to him?'

The man nodded.

'Yes. It is I. I followed him.'

'Why?'

'To tell you to save him. You must save him, lady.'

Rina, breathing hard, stared at the gypsy.

'What do you mean? How can I save him?'

'Gypsies know where you are. They mean to come tonight. They track down Miska and shoot him.'

Rina put a hand up to her hair and brushed it back from her eyes.

'But that can't be allowed,' she said. 'We must find him — warn him. He must escape.'

The man shrugged his shoulders.

'Only you can help him, lady.'

'How can I?'

'By returning, yourself, to Zsil. You must assure him you will go with him to the Castle. Only then will they let Miska go free.'

Rina looked round her wildly. Where was Michael? If only he would come back! He would know what to do.

'Michael!' she called '*Michael!*'

The gypsy sprang forward and held

160

up a warning hand.

'Lady, do not call him. We will not let you do this. He will prefer to die. You must go quietly, secretly, at once.'

'Back to Zsil?'

'Yes. You can follow the trail. It is beaten down by hoof-marks. A horse waits for you on the fringe of the forest.'

Rina tried to think clearly. Her heart pounded with fear — fear for Michael. Her *Miska*. White, stricken, she tried to think clearly. She believed Czico. Why should she doubt him? He was undoubtedly their friend. Why else should he bother to warn them?

Whatever happened, Michael's life must not be risked. That was impossible. Much better that she should go back to Lionel — and ensure her lover's freedom. She loved him. Last night he had made her entirely his. Life had seemed to overflow with passionate sweetness. It was cruelly hard to give it all up, to leave him without even a farewell. But any sacrifice would be worth while if she could save his precious life.

'Czico, is it true?' she besought the gypsy. 'If I go back to the tribe, will they really return me to the Castle and accept Miska as their leader again? Do you swear it?'

The man averted her gaze.

'It is true, lady,' he answered hurriedly. 'Come, I will take you to the horse. Then I will come back here to see Miska and tell him what you have done.'

Rina's eyes filled with tears.

'Very well. Tell him that all my heart is left behind with him and that I shall love him for ever. Tell him I have gone back to the Castle — to save his life; that if he follows or tries to get me back, I will refuse to come and he will merely be executed.'

'Yes, yes.' Czico nodded impatiently. 'Lady, you must hurry or it will be too late to save him.'

The words spurred her on. The gypsy knew that they would. A few minutes later she was standing on the outskirts of the forest. A black horse waited there, tethered to a tree. It was saddled, ready for her.

Czico touched the horse's flank.

'He knows the way back. He will lead you even if you are unsure.'

Rina mounted the horse. Her face was strong, her eyes desperate. She felt that the wound in her heart could never heal. Fate was asking too much. It was sheer agony to be parted from Michael, to be torn so abruptly, so unexpectedly, from his arms. Her body was still warm from his embrace. If only she could see him just once again, hear him tell her that he understood, that he would always remember her as she would remember him, and their wonderful dream of love!

She was white, dry-eyed with misery when at length she rode away. Czico called after her:

'You have saved him, lady, I will tell him all.'

The man's words comforted her a

little. But the chill of death itself seemed to settle on her as she left the green forest behind and rode up the mountain side. She was riding away from all that she loved most in life.

Czico watched until the gallant, graceful young figure on the horse was out of sight. Then he turned and darted away to another part of the forest where a second gypsy waited with two horses. Showing his white teeth in a grin, Czico mounted one of the animals.

'She has swallowed the bait,' he laughed. 'Now come! We are drawing lots for her! Zsil has promised us, brother!'

About ten minutes after the man had ridden away, Michael returned from his expedition. He had a couple of rabbits swinging over the barrel of his gun. He went straight to the tent of boughs and looked in. He was surprised to find it empty. The bed bore the imprint of Rina's body. He bent over the pillow and found it sweet with the fragrance of her hair, an odour familiar, dear and exciting to him. He wondered where she had gone.

He called anxiously:

'Rina, my sweet — Rina, where are you?'

The forest echoed his voice mockingly.

'Rina!' he shouted. 'Rina!'

Once again the only answer was the echo of his own words. Michael picked up his gun. If he fired a few shots she would hear, and know that he had returned. He was lifting the gun to his shoulder when he saw a scrap of paper nailed to the side of the tent. Reaching forward, he picked it up and read the printed words:

I cannot stay. The future is too frightening. Forgive me.

Rina.

Michael stared blankly at the paper. Once again he read the words. His heart seemed to stop beating. The hand which held the paper was numb. It was impossible, fantastic! She had gone! She, who had lain in his arms last night in such complete surrender, under the stars! She, who was part of him! She had fooled him, tricked him once again. With a cry of anger and sorrow, he flung himself face downwards on the ground. He lay like one dead. The words of a song of Heine's, translated from the German, and which he had so often sung, echoed in his ears:

Twice have I loved unhappily,
Twice has love passed me by.
O sun and moon and stars
   — laugh on,
I laugh with you — and die!

He told himself that never again, while he lived, would he love or believe in another woman. But this girl, his wife, with her white witch's body, her red hair and her green, alluring eyes, somehow he and she would meet again. Somewhere there should be redress.

She should pay in full.

What to do now he did not know. At first he decided that he would not return to his people; nor ask them to accept him again as their leader. He would go on alone — become a nomad — one of the wanderers of the tribe. A lone gypsy travelling from country to country with neither kith nor kin, nor home. Without love or tenderness in his life, and with bitterness eating like acid into his soul.

But as he lay there, the desire for vengeance against Rina became so intense within the man. His desire for her was still so acute that he was ashamed of it. Ashamed of loving a woman who was a cheat and a coward.

Yesterday he had thought her gallant, fearless, a woman who would ride with him to world's end and, if need be, share poverty and disgrace with him.

Last night she had never ceased to tell him how much she loved him and how agonized she had been at the thought of marriage with his brother, Lionel.

'I am yours — all yours, for ever, now,' she had whispered again and again, her lips against his ear.

'You will never belong to any other man?' he had asked her. 'You are mine, always mine, from this night onward, aren't you, Rina?'

Her answer had been:

'All yours for always. And I will never belong to any other man. You will never lose me again, my darling.'

Words! Mere words! The facile emotional outpouring of a woman temporarily stirred by passion.

Michael laughed aloud in his bitterness, his face buried in the crook of his arm. His fingers clawed at the leaves upon which he was lying, and his teeth clenched into his lips until the blood came. He hated her. *Hated* her! Yet he loved her. Last night the stars alone were witnesses of how much he had loved her; of how much of his deepest spirit he had given her, as well as his physical adoration.

He was a man of deep reserves, a man who had never before given his soul to a woman. He was humiliated beyond endurance by the thought that he had wasted so much on a red-haired witch who, with the light of day, had been afraid to stay with him; afraid even to face him and tell him, herself, of her change of feeling.

For a long time he lay battling against the insane desire to weep. But of tears he would be too ashamed. When he moved his head, it was only to inhale the fragrance which she had left behind her on that pillow of leaves. The intoxicating perfume of her flame-red hair.

'*Flame of my heart,*' he had called it.

'*A flame which burns only for you,*' had been her reply.

Words. All words! The flickering passion of an hour or two, as light, as ephemeral as the life of a moth.

He heard footsteps and the sound of a woman singing.

Swiftly he raised his head and sprang to his feet. For one mad moment he thought it might be Rina; thought that she might have written that note and hidden just to tease him; that she would return now and spring into his arms, as brave and passionate as ever.

But it was not Rina. It was a dark-eyed, dark-haired girl leading a little grey pack-mule with gay trappings. A girl whom he recognized at once as a gypsy, although not of his tribe.

She was handsome in a coarse fashion; not more than seventeen. She had two raven plaits, full breasts, and bright bold eyes.

'Greetings, brother,' she hailed him in Romany.

He answered in her own tongue.

'Peace be with you, sister.'

With a hand on her hip, she smiled at him.

'All alone in the green forest this lovely morning?'

'Yes,' he said sullenly, 'I'm alone.'

'Then can I eat with you, brother, because I, too, am alone.'

He shrugged his shoulders.

'As you will.'

Her red lips pouted. As she tethered the mule to the tree, she said:

'You have no smile. What ails you, brother?'

'Nothing,' he said roughly; 'nothing at all.'

With a tip of her sandal, she kicked the still warm furry bodies of the rabbits at his feet.

'Two beauties! For your dinner, perhaps?'

'Perhaps!'

'Have you breakfasted?'

'No,' he said.

'Then you shall share mine,' she said. 'I have some cold tea in a can, and some corn-cakes which my grand-mother made only last night.'

Michael sat down, hunching his knees and lacing his arms around them. His face was expressionless and his eyes brooding. He was in no mind for conversation, but neither did he forbid the pretty gypsy to stay awhile and give him a repast. Manlike, he was conscious suddenly of hunger, despite the grief in his soul. Besides, why lie here and moan for a woman who was worthless? He reckoned that this black-eyed child with gypsy blood in her would be faithful to her lover. And if not, according to the fierce law of this country, he would slit her throat.

He sat there in that brooding heavy silence, listening to the girl's light chatter and watching her prepare his meal.

A few minutes later they were eating there side by side, and he was enjoying the good corn-cakes baked by her grandmother.

She did all the talking.

Zingra was her name, she said. She was of a tribe of gypsies who lived north of this forest; where the river flows down to the mouth of the Danube. She had no parents, but her grandmother, who was the queen of the tribe, was her guardian. She had come early into the forest to gather certain berries which the old woman used for brewing a healing tea. Only yesterday she had celebrated her seventeenth birthday. She was a merry child, and laughed continually, her white teeth flashing, her eyes agate-bright. Michael, sore of heart, almost numb from the blow that Rina had dealt him, was unstirred by her physical presence, although she coquetted with him charmingly. But she found the gypsy handsome and fascinating — oh, so much more so than any other man of her own tribe.

She was telling him that she had no lover. Many wanted her but she had no use for them.

'Tell me,' said Michael suddenly, 'if a man had once forged a chain of gold about your neck, taken the Magyar vows to you and danced with you the Magyar love-dance, would you ever leave him?'

Zingra's black eyes grew earnest.

'Never, Miska, never.'

He laughed, and it was a laugh of such bitterness that she did not understand. She took some rice-paper and tobacco from her pocket, and with deft movements of her slender brown fingers, stained red with berry-juice, twisted him a cigarette. She held it out to him.

'No woman could leave *you*,' she said in an insinuating voice.

He took the cigarette and laughed again.

'You are wrong, my child.'

'Have you then been crossed in love?' she asked.

'What does it matter to you?' he asked with sudden roughness.

She looked hurt and disappointed.

'I didn't mean to be inquisitive,' she said.

After all she had done for him, he felt graceless and mean. He reached out a hand and touched her black shining braids.

'You have done no harm, Zingra. You

have been exceedingly kind, and I thank you.'

She made a movement towards him. 'I could do more for you than this.'

For one crazy moment, Michael asked himself why he should turn down what the gods offered. Her full red mouth, luscious as scarlet fruit, was near to his. He bent his handsome head and kissed her. At once, with the passionate abandon of her race, Zingra embraced him. But like a flash he disengaged himself from her arms and stood upon his feet. After last night — and Rina — contact with another woman was abhorrent. White as death, he drew some silver from his pocket and tossed it into Zingra's lap.

'Buy yourself a trinket,' he said hoarsely, 'and keep the rabbits. Thank you, Zingra, my sister, and goodbye.'

The next moment he was on his mount. Turning the animal's head in the direction whence he had come with Rina last night, he rode away into the forest.

Michael's agony of mind was no more acute than Rina's. Weary and sick at heart, she rode steadily back to the gypsy encampment where Zsil awaited her. The horse, intelligent and home-loving, carried her to her destination without a mistake. She had been too blind, too sick with misery to pay much attention to where she was going. Not until she found herself once more outside the gypsy caves on the mountain side did she wake in full to the all-too-acute realization of her position.

The caves were surrounded by an excited crowd of gypsies who shouted in a language she could not understand. They pointed and eyed her menacingly.

Rina slid from the saddle and faced Zsil. She was white and travel-stained, but her loveliness was glorious and undimmed. After last night in Michael's arms in that far-away enchanted forest, some new mature beauty seemed to have been granted her.

'You speak English,' she said.

Zsil bowed low.

'Lady, I do.'

'I have come,' she said, 'because Czico said you would return me to the Castle — and spare Miska's life.'

Zsil did not answer. He looked at her queerly, so queerly that her heart missed a beat and she stared round her uneasily. The encampment was *en fête*. The men were feasting and singing. Zsil's swarthy face was already flushed with wine. Rina added quietly:

'I am ready to go to the Castle.'

Zsil spread out his hands.

'The Castle! Surely you make a mistake?'

Rina's pulses raced with a new, terrible fear.

'But Czico said — '

'Czico, sweet lady, is one of my men. It was at my bidding that he followed you.'

Silence a moment. Her eyes were brilliant now with terror.

'He did not mean to — save Miska?' she gasped.

'No. Only to bring you here,' said

Zsil, and, flinging back his black curly head, laughed loudly. 'Before you return to the Castle, you will help us merry-make — up here.' His hand shot out and gripped hers. 'How do you fancy *me* for a lover, eh, English flower?'

Now she understood. Understood that she had been tricked.

'Let me go!' she cried.

A dozen men gathered round, smiling, talking. Zsil said:

'They are asking that we draw lots for you, lady. How will that assume you?'

Rina, her whole body rigid, looked around her, looked at the brown, fierce faces of the gypsies and saw that their dark, lustful eyes were feasting upon her, that their lips were hungry for her kisses. She stood as if frozen by her fear. To be touched by one of them — she who belonged, body, heart and soul to Michael — it would be a nightmare — unendurable. Suddenly she turned to run, thrusting her hands out blindly.

Half a dozen laughing gypsies caught her. She felt their eager fingers threading through her hair, their wine-laden breath upon her cheeks.

'Let me go!' she screamed. 'Let me go!'

'Do not hurt yourself by struggling, lady,' Zsil laughed. 'See! We draw lots for you. Let us all try our luck. By all the saints in Hungary, it will be a pretty prize for the winner!'

The men shouted with laughter. Rina, held fast by two gypsies, ceased to struggle. It was futile. She was trapped. There was nothing she could do against this wild mob of Magyars.

Each man handed Zsil a strip of paper. He put the strips in a tambourine held by a brown-skinned boy who eyed Rina as eagerly as the rest. Then Zsil turned his back to the crowd.

'On one strip will be written the name of the woman,' he said. 'The man who draws the name will take Miska's bride for his own!'

The crowd roared their approval.

Rina, white as death, looked from one fierce face to another, then shuddered and closed her eyes.

She whispered: 'Michael, my lover. Michael, if you knew . . . '

Zsil turned to the crowd, and the lad shook the papers in the tambourine.

'Draw, all of you! Good luck to us!'

The men drew eagerly. Rina opened her eyes and, with sick horror written on her face, watched each gypsy unfold his strip and look at it.

'No luck, curse it,' said one, and tore up the paper. A dozen others followed suit, grumbling and cursing.

The crowd was too excited to notice their leader draw a strip of paper from his sash. Zsil pretended to open it indifferently. Then his brown, scarred face broke into a smile. He waved the paper aloft.

'Look!' he cried. 'I have won! 'Rina' is written here. I am the fortunate one.'

The others gathered round to look. There was no mistake. Their leader had the winning ticket. They nodded and murmured amongst themselves.

'Ay, Zsil has won. Our luck is out.'

Enviously they watched Zsil take Rina's hand and draw her towards him. Her wonderful beauty, the vivid red of her hair and lips, the marvellous green of her eyes entranced them. Zsil was fortunate.

Rina, the look of dumb horror still on her face, felt Zsil's arms go round her. Then he kissed her lips in front of the others.

'Mine,' he whispered. 'Mine, sweet lady!'

The touch of his lips roused her from her stupor. She struck him with her clenched fist across the face.

'You filthy beast!'

Zsil laughed and, picking her up in his arms, carried her away from the crowd into the cave which had belonged to Miska. He set her on her feet, then sat on the edge of the table and grinned at her. The livid scar across his cheek stood out hideously. He stroked his lip.

'Was I not fortunate to win you, my

English princess? Do not look as though you hated me. Am I not as attractive to you as Miska? You stayed with him here in this cave. Come, give me a kiss. I won you fairly . . . '

'Don't touch me,' Rina said in a low, stricken voice. 'Take me back to the Castle. The Herr Quest will kill you for this!'

Zsil laughed and moved to her side and swung her off her feet, into his arms.

'He will not be given the chance,' he said, his mouth against her ear.

She struggled with him madly, wildly. She would die before she would submit to this treacherous swine. She would die before yielding to any man's embrace. Yes, die here in the very cave where she had once lain in Michael's arms.

Suddenly she felt Zsil's loathsome grip relax. The door of the cave was flung open. A dozen or more gypsies poured in with the sunlight; no longer good-natured and laughing, but with anger and the thirst for vengeance written across their faces.

'Zsil! We want Zsil!' they shouted.

Zsil sprang apart from Rina and drew his knife. He was livid. His eyes rolled. Someone must have seen him draw that slip of paper from his sash. He knew they had found him out — and he knew what they did to one of their own blood-brothers who cheated.

Angry hands caught him and dragged him out of the cave. A storm of fury broke over his head. It was a gypsy girl, jealous of the red-haired Rina, who had told them what he had done. The crowd demanded his blood.

'Liar and traitor!' said one of the men who had himself wanted Rina, and put a knife to Zsil's throat. 'You shall die for this.'

Zsil, craven, terrified, was forced to his feet.

'Kill him,' said a dozen harsh voices.

The knife entered the brown throat of the traitor. Once again, gypsy vengeance was swift and sure.

Rina did not wait to see what was happening to Zsil. In the chaos, the excitement, she knew she must make her escape. She must take advantage of the fact that the attention of the crowd was focussed on the man who had cheated them.

She slid from the shadows of Miska's cave, away, down the mountain side, away from the clamour of the encampment, her eyes wide with terror in her pale young face, her heart beating wildly! She ran desperately. Once or twice she fell over loose stones and thorn bushes, which tore her stockings and ripped her thin shoes. She did not mind. She went on, down the mountain side, through the trees, wildly, like a hunted animal. Anything, anywhere to get away from the gypsies.

Two hours later, exhausted, more dead than alive, she stumbled into the path of a small band of mounted police. Men who were searching, on Lionel Quest's account, for Miska the Gypsy. The search had been in vain. No one in

Foracza had ever suspected that the encampment was in such a wild and remote spot. The police had combed the territory at this altitude, but had not thought it feasible that the camp could be several thousand feet higher up.

The men reined in their horses and stared in astonishment at the figure of the girl, as she staggered through the trees towards them, her clothes torn and stained with blood. She was in a state bordering on collapse.

'Mercy on us,' said one of the Hungarians. 'Look at the colour of her hair. It is the lady of the Castle . . . '

They jumped from their saddles. Kind hands reached out to help her. But they were too late. Rina, with a little moan of weariness and pain, fell fainting at their feet. She awoke, it seemed an eternity, later, to find herself in her soft, luxurious bed in her room at the Castle.

It was late afternoon. A red sunset streaked the sky over the mountains and cast a lurid glow across the gardens. When Rina opened her eyes, the first person she saw was Lionel. He sat by her bedside, his arms folded across his chest, his cold blue eyes fixed upon her.

She gave a long sigh and shuddered. She remembered everything now. Her sacrifice when she abandoned Michael in the forest, thinking that she had saved his life; Zsil's treachery; the men drawing lots for her. It was good to find herself in this soft bed, in this cool, beautiful room with its shaded lamps, and know herself safe from harm.

'Lionel,' she whispered.

He rose at once and stood beside her. His face was a stern mask. When he spoke, his voice was hard and emotionless.

'So you are better, Rina? You have slept for many hours.'

She sat up, wide awake now, and pushed her red, tangled curls back from her forehead. Her relief at finding herself in the Castle changed almost at once to acute misery, an anguish of love and longing for Michael whom she had left in the forest after the glory of their starlit night. She realized that she must tell Lionel now, at once, that she was Michael's wife.

But Lionel was talking.

'I want you to understand,' he was saying, 'that you have disgraced me. You helped Miska to escape, and you accompanied him. Your conduct has been beyond my comprehension. My mother wishes me to send you back to England. But I have made up my mind to keep you here! I married you. I mean you to remain here as my wife. Tonight, Rina, when I come to you, there shall be no drawing back. You have walked out on me once too often. Now I intend to take what belongs to me. If any man attempts to separate us — *I, myself will kill him*!'

Rina looked up at him and saw that the effeminate, haughty Lionel had become, suddenly, a strong, ruthless being. An implacable creature of thwarted passions, determined to conquer her. She trembled, but she spoke to him calmly and quietly.

'I am not your wife, Lionel. I do not belong to you. You have no right to keep me here against my will. It is better for you to take your mother's advice, and send me home. But my home is no longer England. It is *Hungary*.'

He stared at her. His eyes narrowed. His face was sullen and suspicious.

'What do you mean?'

'I mean that I am married to Miska. *His* home is Hungary, therefore it is mine.'

The colour drained from his face.

'You must be crazy, Rina. What the devil are you talking about? You married me . . . here in the Chapel, legally and properly . . . '

'Not legally,' she said, breathlessly. 'I thought Miska was dead when I made those vows to you.'

'Where did you marry him? By what law?'

She lifted the gold chain which lay about her throat, and glittered through the soft chiffon of her nightdress.

'By gypsy law, in his own camp. This is the chain which binds us.'

There was silence for a moment. Lionel stood rigid, staring at her, at the chain. He looked at all her maddening beauty. She was like a lily, he thought, so white and sweet, crowned with the scarlet glory of her hair. The longing for her was in his very blood now. It was intolerable that she should attempt to escape him. Fantastic that she should say she was not his wife, that she was married to that gypsy outlaw.

He suddenly shouted at her:

'I refuse to believe you. I refuse to believe a word you say. You are my wife. No damnable chain about your neck, no futile gypsy law can alter that.'

'I belong to him,' she answered, white-lipped. 'He said so.'

'But I say you do not! I say you are my wife. Tonight I shall come to you — and your door shall be locked. You shall be a prisoner until I come.'

Her face was livid with rage.

Suddenly he leaned over the bed and kissed her, kissed her until she sank back on the satin pillows, gasping, breathless, her eyes dark with rage. Then, laughing, he walked out of the room. 'We shall see later to whom you belong,' he called back.

Lionel, the courteous, the proud — had become a mad tyrant!

Rina heard the key turn in the lock. She lay with closed eyes, her thoughts confused, her body shaken with sobs. How dare he touch her, refuse to believe that she was married to Miska!

She caught at the beloved chain about her throat. The chain which he, her lover, her Michael of the brown, handsome face, the passionate lips and hands, had forged about her neck.

If only she could know the divine peace of last night! That mighty primeval forest, the sweet-scented bed of moss, and know too the curtain of green boughs, the canopy of stars, the music of the birds and of rippling water!

'Michael,' she cried. 'Michael!' and burst into tears.

She was so tired of the struggle and chaos; the mistakes, the misunderstandings. God alone knew where Michael was now. Perhaps the tribe would follow and kill him. Perhaps she would never feel his arms about her again. She did not know how to find him; how to get away from the gilded prison of the Castle. It would be futile to attempt to climb out of the window even if it were possible. Lionel's men would see her and bring her back. Foracza was too small a village to hide in, to pass unnoticed. *She could never get away.*

And Lionel meant to come back — to claim her tonight.

'No, Michael.' She whispered the name of her lover, her true husband. 'No, never! Never any man but you!'

7

It was half past ten that night. The Castle was quiet. Few lights gleamed from the long, narrow windows. The night was warm, windless, moonless, and with the hint of rain in the air.

Rina sat by one of the windows which opened on to her balcony. She sat like a figure of despair, carved from ivory, in her creamy satin wrapper. Her bare feet were thrust in white satin mules, embroidered with silver threads. Every time she heard a noise, a voice in the passage outside her suite, her heart jumped nervously and her cheeks grew hot and red.

Would Lionel keep his word and come tonight to claim her? She believed that he would. Jealousy and passion had transformed this quiet, cold man into a raging tiger. She looked up at the starless sky and wished that she had died last night in Michael's arms, before this could happen to her.

Suddenly she heard footsteps outside her room. The key turned quietly in her door-lock. She jumped up, breathing quickly. When Lionel entered the room, she was standing like a creature at bay, gazing fearfully towards the man who believed himself her husband, who wanted her, madly, despite all obstacles.

He was white, as nervous as the girl herself. But his lips were set in a thin, sullen line. His eyes were hot, red-rimmed. He wore a dark-blue satin dressing-gown which had a heraldic design embroidered in gold above the pocket. His fair hair was brushed smoothly back from his forehead.

Rina looked at him and thought:

'Some women might have wanted him for a lover.'

He reached her side.

'I have come, Rina,' he said slowly. 'I told you I would.' Catching her against him he kissed her hair. 'I want you. I've wanted you for days. Rina, my darling,

you are my wife — you married me
— you belong to me.'

She lay against him and tried to
speak.

'Lionel, I swear before God I am not
your wife!'

He kissed her hair again.

'Yes, you are mine . . .'

She did not struggle. Wearily she
submitted to him. What else was there
to do? But when his lips touched her
mouth and his hands burnt against her
arms, she felt her heart die within her.

Then, suddenly, over his shoulder her
desperate eyes saw the curtains of her
window move apart. Quietly, noise-
lessly, with the grace of a panther, a
man emerged from the balcony into the
warm, scented room.

Rina stared at him. For a moment
she wondered if her eyes were playing
tricks with her. Then she knew it was
true. She gave a little cry.

'You!'

Lionel released her from his arms.
He stiffened and turned round. Then

he, too, saw the tall figure of the gypsy. The man looked tired, haggard, his embroidered blouse torn, his hair matted. He looked as if he was in the final stage of exhaustion, but his black, splendid eyes burnt like fire in his bronzed face.

Michael had, indeed, been half-demented since he had made up his mind to follow Rina. Bitter resentment burned in his heart. He had come with lust for vengeance blinding him to reason.

Rina had no time to speak. She saw Lionel pull something from the pocket of his dressing-gown; something which glittered in the lamplight. At the same moment, Michael drew his knife. Screaming, Rina ran towards Lionel. She knew he was going to shoot. But she was too late. He had raised the gun. There was a blinding flash.

Only when the smoke cleared did Lionel realize what he had done. He had shot Rina. She had run between him and the gypsy. Without a sound, she sank to the floor at his feet, her ivory-satin wrapper spattered with her blood.

The two men ran towards her. Lionel switched on all the lights, flooding the big room with brilliance. He went down on his knees beside her, calling her name, rubbing her hands. Michael did not touch her. He said quietly:

'It's all right. You've only got her through the arm. She isn't badly hurt.'

Lionel made an examination. The gypsy was right. The blood was flowing from a wound just above Rina's right forearm. He took his handkerchief and tied up the arm, feverishly, to stop the flow of blood. Then he looked up and caught the full gaze of the gypsy. For the first time, he saw the intruder closely in the bright light. His heart seemed to stand still.

Then he said, in a voice that cracked:

'*Michael!* Oh, my God!'

The gypsy gave a bitter smile.

'Yes, Lionel.'

'Michael, my *brother*!' Lionel stared

at him, stupefied.

'No, that's forgotten. I am Miska the Gypsy.'

'You, Michael, are that outlaw, that devil incarnate!'

Michael stood up.

'I was always a devil, wasn't I?'

'It's unbelievable,' said Lionel, hoarsely.

'But true. Only don't be afraid. I'm not coming back to disgrace you, my dear fellow. I shall return to the life I prefer — alone.' He looked down at the body of the girl on the floor. 'She's yours, Lionel. Keep her.'

'I simply don't understand . . . '

Lionel was stammering, bewildered. He was reduced to a state of complete mental confusion by the discovery that Miska and his brother were one and the same. He was terror-stricken too, lest Michael meant to come back and tell everybody that years ago he had been unjustly accused and that he, Lionel, had been guilty of the wrong for which Michael was banished.

'Don't worry,' Michael said. 'I'm

going out of your life, Lionel, as I went out once before. Rina has shown which man she prefers.'

Lionel kept silent. He knew that Rina's intention had been to save Michael. He muttered:

'She was my wife — you had no right.'

'No, she was mine,' Michael said, in a low, fierce voice, 'by gypsy law. But I've finished with her. Keep her, Lionel. She has chosen you tonight. I shall never see her again. By gypsy law, I shall separate myself from her, finally.'

He knelt down by the girl on the floor. Rina moaned and opened her eyes but could not see him. He was filled with bitterness when he touched her. He had loved her. But she had chosen Lionel. He would never see her again. Never again would he be tricked and fooled.

'What are you going to do?' Lionel asked, eyeing his brother nervously.

'You'll see,' said Michael, taking a small instrument from his pocket. 'Just give me two minutes, then you will never see me again.'

Lionel shrugged his shoulders.

'But, Michael, see here, if I can do anything . . . '

Michael looked up quickly. His eyes were bright with hatred and scorn.

'You can do nothing. When we were boys, you deliberately tried to ruin me. Keep your position of ease and luxury and virtue, my dear Lionel. I don't want it. You have everything — even the woman I wanted. All I ask is to be allowed to go in peace. Keep your men off me until I am out of Hungary.'

'But, of course, my dear fellow,' said Lionel, in a nervous, humble voice.

Michael was bending over the bed. His brother watched curiously and saw that Michael was fingering the gold chain that was about Rina's neck; doing something to it with the tool in his hand. Lionel could not see the expression on Michael's face — the pain in his eyes, as his hands touched Rina's lily-white throat, and as his gaze drank in, for the last time, the beauty of her face.

Lionel said:

'You won't try to see our mother, will you?'

Michael laughed shortly.

'No. She never had much use for me. It was always you.'

'But I can't see why it was necessary for you to become an outlaw and give all this trouble to the police,' began Lionel.

'To hell with your criticism,' broke in Michael, fiercely. 'Start criticizing yourself, my dear chap. Ask yourself why you and Hannen Vaile, between you, schemed to turn me out of my home. What you did to me, Lionel, was worse than anything I have done since I joined the gypsies.'

Lionel coughed and drew a finger across his lips. He was sweating. He dreaded that someone would find Michael here, recognize him and tell Madame Quest. He knew that in recent years, since their mother had grown older, she had longed to see Michael. She had spoken of him many times, and not unkindly. She had even said that she hoped to see her black sheep of a son before she died. Well, it would not suit Lionel for his brother to come back into their lives. Especially not *now*, since this girl whom they both wanted had shown a preference for *him*.

Michael turned from the bed. His face was a mask. With cold contempt he looked his brother up and down.

'A magnificent bridegroom,' he sneered. 'It is indeed a pity that the bride has been injured. I advise you to have that arm seen to at once. The bleeding has not stopped.'

'Of course, of course,' mumbled Lionel, 'the moment you have gone, I'll get her maid and a doctor. I can say it was an accident. We can hush it up from mother.'

Michael did not look back at the bed, and at the red-haired girl who lay unconscious upon it. All his senses seemed frozen. Without even uttering a goodbye, he left the brother whom he had not seen for years, and the woman whom he had once loved more than life itself.

When Rina recovered consciousness, it was to find the doctor, who had attended her before, probing the wound in her arm for the bullet, and a scared-looking maid, holding a basin, beside her. Lionel, too, was in the room. He was saying:

'Whatever we do, we must keep the truth from my mother, and concoct some plausible story.'

Rina tried to speak, to call for Michael, but gave a cry of agony as the probe entered her arm again, and fainted for the second time that night.

Upon recovering consciousness once more, she was alone with Lionel. Her arm was bandaged and no longer hurt so acutely. The room was dim and quiet. She sat up with a cry, fully aware now of all that had happened and with her brain quite clear.

'Oh, Michael, Michael, where are you?'

'He has gone,' said Lionel in a queer voice.

Rina gave a little groan.

'No, no, *no*!'

She put her hands to her neck. Then she gave another, anguished cry. Her chain was not there. That, too, had gone. Suddenly she saw it on the satin quilt. It had been broken in two pieces.

'Who did that?' she cried hoarsely.

Lionel bit his lip, then handed her a sheet of paper.

'Keep quiet, Rina. Read this.'

With burning eyes, Rina read what was written on a piece of the crested notepaper from her desk.

I have broken the chain of love which bound you to me. I know now it is Lionel Quest whom you prefer. Stay with him. You are his wife. By gypsy law, I made you mine. By gypsy law, tonight, I have divorced you. Goodbye.

M.

Rina read the words feverishly. Then she picked up the chain with a heartrending cry.

'No, Michael! It is not true. It is *you* I love. I am still yours. Michael, Michael, come back!'

Lionel looked down at her. It seemed impossible that Rina should be crying for another man, for Michael, his brother. He felt a wave of injury and anger. How dared she! How had Michael dared to put that chain around her neck and make her his wife? He leaned over Rina.

'For heaven's sake, be quiet, unless you wish to drive me mad!' he said between his teeth.

Rina, careless of what he said, turned her head on her pillow and went on crying. Her arm hurt sharply, but she did not notice the pain. She was only aware of her anguished longing for Michael. She could not believe that he had severed the chain which was equivalent to the wedding ring; that he had left her, *divorced* her according to his laws!

'I can't bear it,' she moaned. 'Michael! Michael, come back!'

Lionel gritted his teeth. It was almost more than he could endure to hear her call upon his brother's name. All his old boyhood's hatred of Michael returned in full force. He no longer felt one pang of remorse for what he had done, nor had the recent meeting with Michael brought back any sense of kinship, of the affection which should go with blood ties. He remembered only that he hated Michael.

How astonishing that this Miska the Gypsy, for whom he, Lionel Quest, and the police, had been searching so feverishly, was his own brother! It was a fantastic story — almost unbelievable. Yet he could well imagine the two being one and the same. Michael had ever been fearless. There had always been a wild streak in him which nothing could subdue.

But stranger still was the fact that the girl who had come out here to marry him, Lionel, should have fallen in love with Michael. Since he had first set eyes upon Rina, Lionel had wanted her. His desire for her was a hundred times more potent now, because he realized that she was passionately in love with Michael.

He heard her crying. It drove him to cold fury. With his eyes glaring, he turned, walked to the bed and took her arm so roughly that she gave a sharp cry of pain.

'Oh, be careful!'

'I'm sorry if I hurt you,' he said, between his teeth, 'but I will not have you lying here crying for that man. Stop it! Stop it, I tell you!'

Shuddering, she lay still, her breath coming in little gasps, her large lovely eyes red-rimmed with fatigue and pain. Somehow or other, she managed to speak:

'Tell me what happened to — *him*.'

'He has gone — that's all.'

'You haven't arrested him?'

'No,' said Lionel with a cold laugh.

'In consideration of your feelings, my dear, I have let him go free.'

'Thank you,' she whispered.

'You can only thank me in one way, Rina.'

Shivering, she turned her face to him.

'You have no right to keep me here. You had much better send me home.'

'I have every right. You belong to me and not to that gypsy outlaw.'

She opened her lips as though to argue, but closed them again. The broken chain, glittering on the satin cover of her bed, caught her eye. That meant a severance of the tie between herself and Michael. She knew that only too well. She knew that she need never expect to see him again. He had gone without even realizing the sacrifice she had made for his sake; without even being able to tell him of Czico's treachery, and Zsil's effort to keep her there in the mountains with him.

She picked up the pieces of chain and held them against her breast in a clenched hand. She no longer made a sound, but the tears rolled heavily down her cheeks. She was drenched in desolation. All hope seemed lost to her. She heard Lionel talking to her again.

'Why don't you make up your mind to submit to this marriage to me and forget this other fellow? Good God — am I not the owner of this castle? Cannot I give you everything that a woman wants? What have you to complain about? What is it that you prefer about this rough criminal who calls himself Miska the Gypsy?'

She did not reply. It would have taken her too long, and would have been too difficult, to have explained to Lionel why she preferred Michael. In a voice of despair, she said:

'I don't wish to stay in Hungary. Surely you can't want an unwilling wife, Lionel? For God's sake, send me back to England.'

He felt defeated. Through this woman, his brother was defeating him and he resented it, bitterly. He stood up, walked back to the window and looked out.

Dawn was breaking over the mountains of Foracza. A red stormy dawn, the horizon streaked with orange and vermilion. There were angry storm-clouds drifting in gloomy purple masses towards the East. The Castle was bathed in the lurid light. It was a peculiarly threatening kind of morning — and stiflingly hot. The atmosphere had a bad effect upon Lionel Quest's nerves. A fiendish desire shook him — a desire to master this woman and, through doing so, become the conqueror of his brother.

'I will not let you return to England,' he said between his teeth. 'I shall regard you as insane, Rina. You shall remain here in the Castle until you have come to your senses again.'

Rina made no answer. She lay exhausted, her hands still clutching the broken links of the gypsy-chain. She was beyond speech when Lionel turned on his heel and left her.

She gave a long, shuddering sigh and

turned her face to the pillow. Tonight, at least, she would have peace. But her tormented heart could know no peace, even though she was alone. She read and re-read Michael's note. What did he mean? He had divorced her, cast her aside, left her forever. Yet she had parted from him that day in the forest, loving him utterly. She had been entirely his. She had sacrificed herself, gone back to the camp with Zsil in order to save his life. Why did he treat her like this in return?

She determined that, at any cost, she must see him once again. She would tell him that she loved him, assure him of her loyalty and devotion. Then, if he wished to cast her off, she would make no further effort to see him.

Lionel meant to keep her in the Castle, to treat her as though she were mad. But he couldn't do that. She must escape, somehow. She shivered at the memory of his furious face, his mad desire for her. She loathed him now. She was Michael's, and to no other man would she ever give herself.

That day Rina refused to stay in bed. She got up after breakfast, in spite of the fact that she felt tired and languid, and her arm hurt badly. Her maid helped her dress. Afterwards, she stood on the balcony, looking over the great sweep of the Hungarian mountains and watched the storm ride up in billowy clouds. She thought:

'Somewhere in these mountains, Michael is hiding. I must find him.'

While she stood there, the door of her room opened and three people entered. Lionel, looking white, grim and determined, his mother, and the Castle physician.

Madame Quest greeted Rina with scant courtesy. She was aghast at the conduct of her son's wife. Lionel had told her part of the story. She was under the impression that Rina had gone crazy over the gypsy and aided and abetted his recent escape. She looked severely and with contempt at the girl.

'You are ill in mind, rather than body,' Madame Quest said sternly. 'You must be well taken care of, Rina.'

'She is a little mad, poor child,' said Lionel, with his chilling smile.

'A little unbalanced, perhaps,' suggested the doctor, smoothly. He knew he would be well paid for supporting the Herr Quest's theory.

'I am perfectly well and perfectly sane,' Rina told them, feeling like a creature at bay.

The three took no notice of her words. The doctor dressed and bandaged her arm. The wound was clean and healing.

'That's better,' he smiled, patting her shoulder.

'I'm absolutely sane,' Rina repeated, shaking off his hand, 'I wish to be allowed to go home to England.'

'You will stay here, where you belong,' Lionel said. 'When you come to your senses you will be treated as an ordinary, normal person again.'

Her eyes flashed at him.

'What do you mean to do?'

'Keep you within bounds of Castle grounds,' he said, coldly. 'It would be not safe for you to go out.'

She tried to laugh, but the laughter ended in a sob. She put a hand against her trembling lips.

'It is you who are mad, Lionel. I won't submit to such treatment.'

'You must do what the doctor thinks best,' Madame Quest said firmly.

'It's a conspiracy,' Rina cried. 'I won't be made a prisoner.'

She ran towards the door of her room, but the doctor stood in front of her.

'Now, now, my child . . . I beg you to keep calm,' he said, soothingly.

Rina tried to push him aside. Lionel's hands gripped her shoulders and drew her back.

'You see, she is quite crazy,' he said to the physician.

The doctor shrugged his shoulders and left the room — Madame Quest walked with him, tapping on her stick, whispering to the old man.

Rina, trembling with rage and fear, faced Lionel.

'You can't do this to me, Lionel. You must set me free. I won't be treated like a lunatic.'

His eyes narrowed. He smiled unpleasantly.

'You will be treated differently, as soon as you make up your mind to take your rightful place as my wife. The sooner you make up your mind to love me, the better it will be for you — otherwise you remain — a lunatic, my dear!'

Rina did not answer. Lionel turned on his heel and walked slowly from the room. Her heart beat frantically with rage and fear. She went back to her balcony. How close it was. There would be a storm soon. Thunder growled in the distance, threateningly.

Down below, she suddenly noticed a man standing in the garden. He was one of the Castle servants. He had been placed there, she supposed, to watch

— to prevent her from escaping.

She stared blindly at the dark brooding mountains.

'Michael,' she said, in a desperate voice. 'What can I do?'

Lionel's words haunted her.

'*The sooner you make up your mind to love me, the better it will be for you.*'

She knew that she could never love him, that she could only hate him. She wished to God, now, that she had never come out here, even for her family's sake. She wondered what they would think at home if they knew what she had been through, the drama, the tragedy of it all. How could she go on writing normal, cheerful letters to help and comfort them? If only she had never come here.

But no! She could not wish she had never come to Hungary. For it was Michael's country. On that barge, sailing down the Danube, she had met and loved him. She could never forget *that*.

But she knew that unless she saw him

once more and told him that he had wronged her, she would never know another hour's happiness.

Not until much later that night did she see any ray of hope. It had been a black, grim day, remarkable for one of the most violent thunderstorms of the year. The lightning playing continually over the mountains and the incessant crashing of thunder had torn Rina's nerves almost to shreds. But she had not sent for Lionel nor wanted his company. She preferred to sit alone through the racking hours of the storm. Now it was calm. Night brought peace and a full moon to Foracza.

About ten o'clock, Rina heard footsteps outside her room and looking towards the door, saw that a note had been pushed underneath it.

For a moment she thought wildly that it might be from Michael. Running across the room, she tore open the envelope. But she knew at once that it was not from her lover. It was from

Hannen Vaile — Lionel's trusted secretary.

I know the whole circumstances, (she read). *I will help you if you will swear silence and secrecy in return. I can arrange convoy for you back to England. If you wish this, go out on your balcony and let my messenger see the light from your window.*

H.V.

Rina read the note eagerly. She almost laughed. She knew only too well that Vaile was not Lionel's friend, that the man hated his employer. Well, if he could help her, she would let him! She would clutch at any straw. She knew the secretary was all-powerful in the Castle, that he could do anything he wished. Without further hesitation, she opened her windows wide and stepped on to her balcony.

Vaile worked swiftly. Within ten minutes he was in Rina's room. He

217

found her looking ill and miserable — in a state of acute depression and frayed nerves.

'I must get away — I must,' she kept saying.

He put a hand to his black, well-trimmed beard and looked at her through half-shut eyes.

'So! You wish to go home?'

'Yes, yes, back to my own people.'

Vaile smiled and nodded. That suited him admirably.

Michael had been disposed of. Rina had never lived with Lionel and it was expedient that she should be removed before she did so. There must be no heir to the Quests. Vaile meant to take a risk on this thing — a big risk. But if he could get Rina away to England, without being found out, he would be threequarters of the way toward his ambitious goal. There would only be Lionel to deal with — and, after all, Lionel might vanish mysteriously in the near future. Why not? After that, he, Hannen, would have supreme power and most of the money.

'Listen,' he said to Rina. 'I can and will arrange for you to leave Hungary. I will do it tonight before Lionel has time to make further plans for you.'

Rina's hopes began to soar. She clasped her hands together and looked at Vaile with shining eyes.

'Do you mean that?'

'I do,' he said. 'There are a dozen men in this Castle who are in my confidence. I shall see that those particular men are posted as your guards tonight. Once you are outside the Castle walls, a car will await you. You will be driven across the mountain road to Sparitza. From there, you can pick up a German barge which will take you down the river to Vienna.'

Rina closed her eyes and nodded. She knew about those barges and that river. Her heart, which had been so dead, so full of despair, thrilled with fresh pain and longing for Michael. She did not know whether to trust Hannen Vaile or not. But she would say nothing.

She had her own plan. Once she was outside these walls, she would escape from *him*, as well as from the Quests. For of course she did not want to go back to England. She wanted to find Michael.

'You will promise to do as I say?' asked Hannen.

'Yes.'

'Then you must be ready at midnight,' he said, moving towards the door. 'I will go now and give orders to my men.'

Rina moved excitedly about the room, making her preparations. She packed a small case with necessities, took what money she had, and a few jewels. The stiffness and pain in her arm was forgotten. Her whole mind was concentrated on her escape, and how to elude Hannen, once she was outside the Castle.

Restlessly she paced her room. She had put out all the lights. Only a shaft of pale moonlight pierced the gloom. Now and then, she stood at the balcony windows and stared impatiently at the starry sky and the shadowy outline of the mountains.

If only she knew where Michael was! Her heart failed her when she considered the fact that she might never find him, that he might be lost to her for ever.

'I *must* see him once,' she kept saying to herself. 'I must put things right between us, even though he never sees me afterwards.'

She was distracted with anxiety lest Vaile, powerful, though he was, might fail in his plans for her escape. She knew that if she stayed here another twenty-four hours, all would be lost. Lionel would never again be cheated. And she was determined to die before he could force her into his arms.

When midnight struck she was in the last stages of nervous excitement. Then she heard the faint sound of the handle of her door turning. The colour leapt to her cheeks. Her pulses thrilled. The door opened and a man-servant entered the room.

'The Herr Vaile waits,' he said, softly.

Rina hurried into the quiet corridor. It was dark and silent in the Castle. She followed the man down a long, winding staircase, along a subway and up a flight of stone steps which led to a part of the Castle grounds called 'Monk's Walk'.

The moon shone brilliantly, the tall trees cast ghostly shadows on the smooth lawns and clipped hedges. It was cold and a bitter wind blew down from the snow-capped mountains. Rina shivered and hurried along. Hannen's man leading the way.

Five minutes later she found herself outside the great wrought-iron gates, in the roadway. She was exalted by the idea that she was, in a measure, free; that she was away from the Castle which had been a gilded prison, and a horror to her. But her troubles were not over. She still had Vaile to deal with.

She found him standing beside a long black Mercédès. He wore a dark overcoat, and muffler, and his hat was drawn well over his eyes.

'Good,' he said when she reached him. 'Now for Sparitza and the river. So far we are fortunate, my child. Come, get into the car.'

Rina hesitated. The intolerable longing for Michael possessed her. She must get away from Vaile and the car long before they reached Sparitza, which was twenty miles away.

She stared out of the car as the driver accelerated along the rough road which led from the Castle through the mountains. She felt like an actress in a strange drama. It was all queer and sinister. Her face was pale in the bright moonlight, her hands ice-cold.

'I am very grateful,' she murmured to Vaile.

He handed her a roll of notes.

'I am glad to help,' he said. 'Here is money for your fare. I only ask you to promise that you will never return to Hungary, or see Lionel again.'

'I promise that,' she said, and meant it.

They neared the triple crossroads, one of which led to Foracza, the other into the mountain pass for Sparitza, and one, a narrower road, which led up to the mountains in the direction of the gypsy camp. She looked at it and thought:

'If I took that road I could find the path to the camp, and somewhere I should find *him*!'

Suddenly she gave a little cry and leaned against Vaile's arm.

'What's the matter?' he asked, anxiously.

'I feel ill,' she gasped. 'I think I'm going to faint.'

He put an arm round her shoulder.

'Try to pull yourself together,' he said, urgently. 'We must get ahead.'

'Water,' said Rina, weakly. 'If I could just have some water.'

Vaile cursed under his breath and called to the driver.

'Stop,' he said, angrily. 'I must find water — the lady has fainted.'

He jumped from the car, swearing at

himself for being a fool. He had brought a flask with him, but it was empty. He had meant to fill it with brandy. It was like the wretched girl to faint at this moment.

Rina watched him run towards a mountain stream which they had just passed. The chauffeur was hunched sleepily over the wheel. This was her chance! Flinging off the heavy fur coat in which she had been wrapped, she stepped swiftly out into the road.

Breathlessly she ran up the mountain side, further and further away from the car. She laughed to herself, her eyes bright as the stars. She had outwitted Vaile. Now she was free, free to find Michael, even though she must walk to world's end!

Vaile returned to the car with a flask of water. Then he stopped. The flask dropped from his hand. White with amazement and fury, he saw that the car was empty. Rina had gone!

Furiously, he shouted at the driver.

'Get down, you fool! Get down, I say,

and help me find her, unless you want a bullet through your head!'

The two men looked in every direction. Vaile, livid with rage, kept shouting her name.

'Rina! Rina! Where are you?'

There was no answer. Only a mocking echo from the starlit mountains, and the sudden hoot of an owl in the shadowy trees. Vaile continued the search for half an hour. But it was hopeless. She had vanished as mysteriously as though the earth had opened and swallowed her. She was on none of the main roads, and she had the advantage of the darkness and the vastness of the territory. It was a vain task, here, in these mighty Hungarian mountains.

Vaile wiped his forehead, which was bathed in perspiration, and returned to the car. He ordered the driver to turn and drive home. It was useless to wait any longer.

'The red-haired devil,' he muttered to himself. 'She will pay for this if we ever meet again.'

Where had she gone? Why had she done this? There could be only one answer. She had gone to find Miska.

He lit a cigarette and smoked furiously as the car sped back towards the Castle. He could know no peace as long as the girl whom Lionel desired was in the country. And he feared that there would be some awkward moments for him when Lionel discovered that she had escaped.

Vaile's fears were well founded. Lionel found out next morning that Rina had gone, and rushed to his mother. Madame Quest was secretly pleased. She only hoped that the girl who had destroyed her son's reason and happiness had vanished for ever. But Lionel was like a madman. He raged round the Castle, threatening to have everyone shot or put in irons in the dungeons.

How had Rina passed her guards? Not a man in the Castle had an explanation or excuse. A strange secrecy and dumbness prevailed. Upon nobody could the blame be attached. Least of all did Lionel suspect that Vaile, his friend and secretary, had anything to do with it. The man's duplicity and subtlety never entered his master's head.

Lionel realized that, somewhere, he was the victim of treachery. He was, however, more concerned with finding Rina again than with punishing traitors. The very fact that the girl had been denied him, again and again, put the devil itself into him.

He would possess that maddening grace and beauty — or die for it!

8

Rina soon found the beginning of the path which, she knew, led up to the gypsy encampment. Below, she could hear the shouts from Hannen Vaile echo and die away. Her heart seemed to burst with its frantic beating. Her face was strained with fear, but she rushed on, straining every limb, her love and longing for Michael giving her strength. It was hard work climbing the mountain. The pathway was dark and torturous. Now and then, the brilliant moonlight pierced through the trees and helped her. Every sound, every hoot of an owl startled her and sent the blood rushing through her body. Sometimes, she stumbled and fell, bruising her legs and arms. Her stockings were ripped to shreds, her thin shoes cut through by sharp stones. She did not care. Her only thought was to go on, to find Michael.

'Michael!' She kept saying the beloved name. Michael was her goal. She must find him, explain everything.

She realized that he might not be with his people. She might never find him. She might be going back to the terror of the gypsies, a terror from which she had only just fled. But love gave her courage and lent her wings. She went on until her senses swam with fatigue and she felt sick and exhausted. Only by a superhuman effort could she force herself to continue the climb.

At last she could go no further. For two solid hours she had been struggling upwards. She sank down to the ground and lay panting, with eyes closed. Almost at once she was asleep. She had reached the stage of complete collapse.

She awoke to find the sun shining brightly and to hear the birds singing. She was reminded of that waking in the green forest, after the enchanted night with her lover. The tears filled her eyes. She rose to her feet, brushed the leaves and twigs from her hair, stretched cramped and aching limbs and whispered:

'Michael, beloved, I must go on!'

She continued to climb. She was stiff and sore, but physical pain could not deter her. She was following her man, with the strange fortitude which love gives to a woman.

At last she reached the heights, thousands of feet above Foracza, and saw the wild, lonely encampment of the gypsies.

Her heart beat madly. Her eyes, bright and eager, rested upon a scene of great activity. The camp seemed to be *en fête*. Gypsies swarmed in and out of their caves. There was the sound of music and singing, of tambourines and of voices raised in an impassioned chant.

Rina, her face white and weary, her hair tangled and wild, mingled with the crowd. Then she heard a great shout go up:

'*Miska! Miska!*'

A wave of ecstasy beat in her brain. She thanked heaven for the instinct which had led her to climb the mountain. Michael was here. She had not come in vain. He had returned to his people.

She pushed her way through the crowd of gypsies who were dancing and singing in the hot sunshine. It was a glorious fresh morning. The sun glittered on the white peaks which were covered by the perpetual snows. The slopes were brilliant with spring flowers, carpeted with alpine plants of vivid blue and scarlet and gold.

On the grass plateau where, that night which seemed so long ago, she had been united by gypsy law to Michael, a man sat on a carved chair. Rina's eyes rested on him and her lips formed his name:

'*Michael!*'

It was good to see him after that terrible climb, to know that at last she was within reach of him.

Soon she would be able to explain

everything, and he would take her in his arms and make her forget the nightmare, the horrors through which she had passed.

She feasted her gaze on him. How splendid he was in his Hungarian costume with brilliant embroidered tunic, and scarlet sash! He looked brown and strong. She was too far away to see the hard set of his lips, the intense weariness and sadness in his eyes.

Rina pressed closer to the platform. Why did he sit there like a king about to be crowned? Then she saw that a girl was sitting at his feet. A beautiful, dark-eyed gypsy in her National Festive costume. She had a wreath of scarlet flowers in her hair, gold ear-rings, and on her bare brown arms were a dozen or more gleaming bangles of beaten silver and gold.

The eagerness died from Rina's eyes. A cold feeling clutched her heart. That girl, and Michael — why were they there together? Rina knew who she was.

She had often seen her in the camp. Pepita, they called her, the prettiest girl in the tribe.

Silence fell upon the crowd. The music and dancing ceased. Michael rose to his feet. Pepita stood with him and he took her hand and lifted her up beside him. Then he held up his other hand and something flashed in the sunlight. Rina's eyes fastened upon it. She knew what *that* was. It was a chain, a gold chain similar to the one which Michael had put about her neck. The wedding ring, symbol of the gypsy marriage. *He was about to marry Pepita!*

Something in Rina's heart seemed to die. After the agony of wanting Michael, after all her loyalty and devotion, it was more than she could endure to witness his marriage to another girl. She could, *would* not see that chain placed about Pepita's brown, strong, young neck.

Madly, Rina pushed through the crowd, fighting to reach the platform.

Her shrill, anguished voice broke the silence:

'Michael! *Michael!* Stop!'

Michael started violently. The chain fell from his fingers and he dropped Pepita's brown hand. He searched the crowd with his eyes. Then he saw Rina, her face white and exhausted, her hair dishevelled. He stared at her as though stupefied.

'Rina!'

A murmur went up from the gypsies. They watched the slim figure of a red-haired girl reach the platform and drop to the ground. They recognized her now. It was the English girl from the Castle! What was she doing here?

Michael leaned down and lifted Rina on to the platform beside him. He murmured her name, 'Rina — *Rina!*'

His mind was utterly confused. He had been trying hard to forget her, to wipe out all memory of their love. He believed, after the scene in the Castle, that she loved Lionel, that it was Lionel whom she had tried to save from *him*;

that she was content to remain there as Lionel's wife. So he had severed the chain and divorced her from him. His heart was broken, but he wished to return to the gypsies whom he had once loved and to whom he had once been a well-loved leader.

He had found them in confusion. Zsil murdered; Czico out of favour. The gypsies chaotic, like lost children without a leader. They could trust nobody. Every man's hand seemed to turn against his brother. Like children, they needed guidance.

When their former favourite Miska appeared, they acclaimed him wildly. They had been led astray by the traitor, Zsil. They were remorseful and eager to make amends. Nobody had led them so well as Miska. In his time they had been a happy, contented people.

Michael was swept along on a tide of enthusiasm and popularity. Last night there had been peace, for Miska was weary and depressed and they had left him to sleep. But this morning there was to be feasting and rejoicing.

At midday he was claimed once more as their king and leader. Every hand was raised in allegiance, every man and woman swore loyalty and obedience. And the popular wish was that he should settle down to marriage with Pepita, who had always loved him and who was the young queen of beauty in their camp. So Michael did as they asked of him.

It was to please his clamouring people that he agreed to take Pepita as his wife. Only to please them. He wanted no wife, no woman in his heart. He had loved Rina and he would never love again. His heart had died on the night he took the chain from her throat — so he had imagined. But now he knew that his heart had not died within him. He was neither lifeless nor hopeless. His body and brain were filled with the old wild fever, the old passion for Rina. He drew her on to the platform and looked aghast at her pale face, her feet which were covered with blood.

'Why are you here? In God's name, why did you come — and how?'

She looked up at him and smiled. Then she said in a low, faint voice:

'Michael — I am so tired!'

'Oh, Rina, my poor darling!'

The words burst from him. He had sworn never again to use the word 'darling', never to let his senses swim for any woman. But they were swimming now, as he put an arm around her and guided her to his chair. He seemed oblivious of the crowd, of the hundreds of people who watched them. He did not hear Pepita when she called his name. Pepita, whose brown pretty face was ashen and aghast at this terrifying interruption to her bridal.

'Rina,' he said again, and wiped her delicate torn feet with his scarf. 'What does this mean?'

'It means that I love you. I followed you . . . I climbed the mountains to find you.'

'In God's name — why? You left me in the forest. You wished to return to Lionel.'

'No, it was you I loved. You I have always loved.'

'But you tried to save him from my knife.'

She shook her head.

'No, I tried to save *you* from *his* bullet.'

'But you ran away! You left me in the forest,' he repeated wildly.

'You are wrong again, Michael,' she said, and smiled again that tired, tragic smile. 'I would have died in your arms rather than have left you. Czico fooled me. He told me that if I did not leave you, the gypsies would find and kill you. I wanted to save your life. I went with him in order to save you and he promised to tell you what I had done — and why.'

There was silence. Michael, his eyes glowing, stood like a statue, motionless, transfixed. The light of understanding was breaking over him. Yes, he understood everything now. He saw how bitterly he had wronged her. Her love for him had been no less than his for her. She had been loyal to the end. She would have sacrificed herself to spare his life.

A cry broke from his lips:

'Oh, Rina, Rina beloved, forgive me.'

She leaned her cheek against his hand and kissed it.

'My dear, it has been worth it, just to reach you and hear you call me by that name again.'

He put a hand to his eyes. They were wet. Then he realized that Pepita was close to them, speaking to him, beseeching him.

'You are mine, Miska,' she said. Her large black eyes were aflame.

He turned to her and spoke gently.

'No, Pepita. No, little sister, I am not yours. I was about to do you a great wrong, and this *goy* an even deeper one. I belong to her. She is my wife.'

'You divorced her,' Pepita began to sob, and disappointment filling her heart, for she was madly in love with the handsome leader.

'Unjustly,' he said. 'It is written in our law that no man shall divorce his wife without good cause. I thought she had betrayed me. But it is I who betrayed her.'

He turned back to Rina. White and still, she was sitting beside him, her eyes shining. The sun touched her hair to golden-red. She said:

'Thank God I got away from the Castle. Oh, my dearest, I am happy only when I am with you.'

He smiled and took her hand.

'Then you will always be happy!'

A cry went up from the people. A dozen voices clamoured. The men argued and protested. Miska had sworn to abandon the red-haired *goy*, to take their own Pepita for his wife. Was he already going back on his word to them?

Rina could not understand their grumbles and complaints, but she guessed that they resented her return.

'Shall I leave, Michael — until they

calm down?' she asked.

'If you go, I go with you,' he said quietly.

The tears rolled down her cheeks. She shut her eyes and thought:

'It was all worth while, to hear him say those words.'

Michael raised a hand and silenced the people. He began to speak to them in their own language. He spoke fervently, impassionedly. The gypsies listened in respectful silence. He was a magnificent orator. His words seemed to hold them spellbound, to cast a spell over them.

In their own romantic language, he told them the story of his love for the English girl, how he had misjudged and hurt her. He told them of her devotion and fidelity when Czico had betrayed her; how, without just cause, he, Miska, had cast her from him. He spoke of her difficult, perilous journey to him, that climb from Foracza which even the strongest man in the camp usually attempted on horseback.

Michael knew that these people were essentially romantic. He knew that they would respond to the story of passionate love which he endowed with all the rich beauty of their own emotional, picturesque folk-tales. When he had finished, there was not a dry eye among the women, and the men stood with heads bowed, a look of shame on their faces. He had them under his sway. There was not one, save Pepita's parents, who protested or argued.

'Rina of the Red-Hair is a worthy mate for your leader,' Miska ended passionately. 'Has she not shown courage and strength of will and undaunted spirit? Did she not sacrifice herself for me when Czico, at the bidding of the traitor, Zsil, came in pursuit of me? Listen, my people! If you will accept this woman as my true wife, to bear me sons who will take my place when I am dead, I will stay amongst you. I will lead and rule you loyally and wisely while there is breath in my body. But if you will not accept her, then I must go and take her with me. She is my wife. Now that I know the truth, no other woman can take her place. You must choose!'

With one accord, the gypsies shouted back to him:

'We will accept Rina of the Red-Hair. Stay with us, Miska. Do not leave us again. We cannot find peace and happiness without you.'

A great light sprang to Michael's eyes. Radiant, he turned to the girl who sat beside him.

'Sweetheart,' he said, 'look up and smile. They have chosen you.'

Lifting her from the chair, he picked up the gold chain which had been prepared for Pepita, and put it about Rina's throat. Then he signed to a gypsy to step forward. The man handed him a red-hot tool and Michael swiftly forged the links together.

Rina did not speak. She was speechless with happiness and emotion. Her pride in him was limitless. She could only look at him with all her soul's love in her eyes. The golden links were forged again. This time the chain would never be taken off. When she died, it would be buried with her, still unbroken about her neck.

When the shouting of the tribe had died down, Michael lifted Rina in his arms and carried her to his cave. There it was cool and dim and sweet-scented with Spring flowers. The couch was covered with a mass of pure white mountain lilies. Very gently, Michael laid her down upon them. They were crushed under her weight, and gave out a sweet, subtle perfume. Kneeling beside her, he took both hands in his and kissed them.

'My own precious Rina!'

'Is it true?' she whispered, her arms about his neck. 'Is it really true that I am with you again?'

'Yes, sweetheart — quite true.'

'And you know now that I love you?'

'I know it,' he said, kissing her hair. 'I don't deserve your lips, beloved.'

Her eyes shone at him. Her hands

drew the handsome head close to hers.

'But I want you to kiss my lips. They are yours.'

Bending over her, he touched her warm red lips with his. Then he brought a bowl of water and some strips of linen. As gently as a woman, his sensitive fingers touched her cut feet and bruised ankles. He bathed and covered them with ointment before bandaging them. He made a sling from a striped silk gypsy scarf for her injured arm.

Dumb with happiness, she lay on her bed of flowers and watched him. One by one he took off her torn clothes. Bathed her with warm water, combed the tangled red glory of her hair. A thick white silk shawl, embroidered with violet silks, lay across the end of the couch. Michael wrapped it round her slim body and put a cushion behind her head. He would not let her do anything for herself. He seemed to take a delight in being maid as well as lover to her.

When he had finished, he sat back and looked at her. He thought he had never seen a woman look so lovely. The expression in her eyes stirred his very soul.

'Now,' he said, 'my darling, *darling*, I shall be your lover as well as your slave.'

His arms went around that warm white body and hers about him. They were locked in a wild, sweet embrace, heart beating against heart, lips clinging, hungry for the kisses so long denied them.

They were one again. Husband and wife by gypsy law; lovers, according to love's law.

When the flame of their passion had flickered down to tenderness, Rina looked into his brilliant eyes and sighed deeply.

'Poor Pepita,' she whispered, 'I can pity her.'

'She will forget,' he said. 'She never loved me. She was a mere child.'

'She will never know love as you have taught it to me. No man will ever inspire in her that tremendous passion you have inspired in me. Michael, she has lost what I now hold dearer than life.'

'I never belonged to her,' he said. 'Had I married her to please the people, I would only have hated her tonight. I would never have loved her as I love you, my darling. My love is for you only. All for you.'

She made no answer, but kissed his eyes and his throat, threading her fingers through his thick, dark hair. The hours passed swiftly. Hours which she could never forget. Not until evening did they leave their cave and join the gypsies.

The tribe was still making merry, celebrating the wedding of their leader. Sitting outside their cave, Michael and Rina watched the splendour of the red sun sinking behind the purple mountains. It pleased the people to see them there and speak with them. They were delighted because Rina, lovely and like a gypsy-queen in her white shawl, with white roses in the red of her hair, said a few halting words to them, in their own language.

Darkness had fallen and the men's torches were alight before their peace was disturbed by the return of a gypsy from Foracza. The man was riding madly up the mountain side.

'News, master,' he said when he stood, panting, before Michael. 'Grave news.'

'What is it, Perenzo?'

'The lord of the Castle is dead.'

Michael drew a hand across his face.

'The Herr Quest? You are sure?'

The man nodded.

'Yes, Miska. He was found murdered. Hannen Vaile, the secretary, has been arrested. The mother of His Excellency is said to be dangerously ill.'

Michael turned slowly towards Rina. For a moment he was silent, then he repeated Perenzo's words in English.

She gazed at him with dilated eyes.

'Michael, how horrible!'

'We must go,' he said tersely.

'Go where?'

'Down to the Castle.'

Rina stepped back with a little cry.

'To the Castle?' she repeated. 'But why, Michael? It would do no good. Surely it would . . . '

Michael took one of her hands and looked into her eyes.

'I must tell you now, Rina. You must know. My real name is Michael Quest. I am Lionel's brother.'

9

For a long while Rina stared dumbly at the grave face of her gypsy lover. He was her husband, her mate; king of the mountains, of the green forests and wilds of Hungary. But surely, *surely* not one of the Quests!

She put a hand to her forehead in a confused way. She had a swift mental vision of Lionel; the weak, fair man with his cold, stubborn personality. She could not reconcile herself to the fact that the two men were brothers.

Then she heard Michael's voice:

'Come, Rina, it is true, my darling. We must go to the Castle immediately. Perenzo, saddle my horse and find one for my wife.'

The gypsy ran to do his master's bidding. The others crowded anxiously around their leader. Rina could not understand. But Michael's word was law. What he wished her to do, she would do. If he wished her to go to the Castle with him, she would go.

Once again Michael spoke to his people in their own picturesque language. They listened with astonished interest to what he said.

Years ago, when as a slim, handsome youth, he had joined their wandering tribe, later to become their leader, none had known whence he had come. They had only learned, quickly enough, that he was brave, clever, educated, a natural king, and one who spoke to them in their own tongue as though he had been born of them.

Now they learned that he was Michael Quest, brother of the High Excellency of the Castle, and rightful heir to the vast possessions, the great wealth of the Quests. He told them that he had been unjustly accused of a sin which he had never committed, that he had severed all ties with his home and family, and become a gypsy; taking the name of Miska.

Now his brother was dead, and his mother was dying. The call of blood was stronger than the vow he had taken to the gypsies years ago that he would never be reunited with his own people. He must see his mother, he said, and make peace with her before she died.

The gypsies understood. Their sympathies were with their leader. But there was a childlike, dumb anxiety in the dark eyes which were fixed in his direction. A white-bearded old man came forward.

'Do not leave us, Miska,' he said sadly. 'Do not abandon us for the people of Foracza. We are as lost sheep without your guiding hand.'

Michael's features softened. He raised his hand.

'I swear loyalty and allegiance to my people,' he called. 'I will return.'

Perenzo brought the horses. Michael's chestnut mare, and a sturdy mountain pony for Rina. Together they rode down the sunlit mountain side, the gypsies shouting words of encouragement.

Not until the sound of voices had died away and they were alone, skirting the narrow pathway between the tall trees, did Michael speak. Then he touched his young wife's shoulder and looked at her with great tenderness.

'It is good of you to come with me,' he said. 'Good of you not to question or reproach me.'

'I love you,' she said simply.

He smiled.

'My own darling. Now I will tell you everything.'

While they rode, the horses picking their way down the tortuous descent which was streaked with sunshine and leaf-shadow, Rina heard the whole story of Michael Quest. She heard it half in sorrow, half thrilled. She was sorrowful for his sake because the impulsive, passionate boy had been misjudged and misunderstood. She was thrilled by the thought that he had made his own way in life, that he had become a king, a leader of men.

'Perhaps I was wrong not to tell you

before,' he finished. 'But I wanted to forget.'

'I understand.'

His arm went around her. They rode together in intimacy and sympathy.

'You understand everything!'

Rina looked into his eyes.

'But I find it difficult to comprehend how two brothers could be so utterly different. Poor Lionel! When I met him in England and he asked me to marry him, I knew I could never really love him. I agreed to marry him for my family's sake. It was wrong of me. I never knew love until I met you.'

'Nor I till I met you.' He looked at the glory of her hair gleaming in the sunshine. 'Flame-colour,' he whispered. 'Colour of my heart's blood.'

Rina's eyes were blurred by tears of ecstasy. Such happiness as this was more than she had ever hoped for.

She talked to him of the old chatelaine of the Castle.

'Is your mother dangerously ill?' she asked.

Michael nodded.

'Perenzo says so. I want you to see her, to tell her of our happiness.'

'I will tell her, too. I want her to like me. She did not care much for me when I was there with Lionel. I could never be natural in the Castle — I was so wretched, so frightened.'

'This time you go there as my wife, and the new mistress of the Castle,' he said quietly.

'No. I will remain Miska's wife,' she smiled. 'I will always be the wife of Miska the Gypsy.'

They did not speak again until they came to the Castle gates. Slowly they rode through the spacious grounds up the velvet grass slopes, past the white terraces to the grey battlements. Then Michael, looking up, saw the flag of his ancestors still flying high, rippling in the breeze.

'My brother is not dead!' he exclaimed.

A groom came running up and saluted.

'No, Excellency. But he is at death's door.'

Rina felt the colour leave her cheeks. Lionel was still alive! She would have to see him, speak to him! She was pale and trembling when Michael led her through the great hall of the Castle. The room with its dark, heavy tapestries and stained-glass windows seemed more than usually gloomy and forbidding. The atmosphere of solemnity and tradition struck a chill in her heart. But she followed swiftly behind Michael up the winding staircase where two doctors and nurses waited to take them to the room where Lionel was lying.

The Castle physician, that same man who had attended Rina after her collapse, gave Michael the news. He said that Lionel's vitality was ebbing. The wound in his back, which had pierced a lung, had proved fatal. But Madame Quest was better and wanted to see her younger son.

Michael and Rina walked to the great four-poster bed. Shivering, Rina looked at the man who lay there on the pillows. Lionel was waxen-white, his breath came quickly, his fair hair clung damply to his forehead. But a look of relief lit up his sharpened features when he saw them.

'Michael!' he said. 'Rina!'

Michael took his hand.

'I just heard, Lionel. We came at once.'

'It was Vaile,' Lionel said faintly, a smile twisting his thin lips. 'My *friend!*'

'How did it happen?'

With difficulty Lionel Quest told his story. He had awakened that morning to see a figure in his room; had tried to get his revolver but he was too late. Vaile had fired first. The servants caught the secretary trying to escape into the corridor.

Michael looked gravely at his brother.

'I always knew Vaile was a traitor, Lionel. But tell me, what can we do for you?'

'Nothing, I am dying. Just say that you forgive me — for everything — that's all.'

Michael laid a gentle hand on his brother's arm.

258

'I forgive you gladly.'

Lionel turned his eyes that were fast glazing towards the woman he had so passionately desired.

'And you, Rina. You must forgive me and believe me when I say I am glad you found your — gypsy lover.'

'Thank you, Lionel,' she said. The tears were welling fast into her eyes. 'But I am the one who should ask your forgiveness. I — '

'It was my fault,' Lionel broke in. 'I have told my mother the truth about — the girl who died. She knows now and everybody else will know soon that I was guilty and that Michael was wrongfully accused.'

Suddenly his face changed. A spasm of pain shuddered through his body. Turning to the doctor, Michael took Rina's hand and led her from the room.

★   ★   ★

That evening when the sun set behind the mountains, and the grounds of the

Castle were dyed red by the last fiery rays, Rina walked on the white terrace, alone, save for the two graceful wolf-hounds that had been Lionel's favourite dogs, and which followed her everywhere.

She paused to look up at the Castle. The flag was flying at half-mast. Foracza was in mourning. The High-Excellency was dead. Tomorrow he would lie in state so that his people might pass through the flower-filled room and pay their last respects.

In Madame Quest's bedroom, Rina knew, a reunion was taking place between the mother and her younger son.

Madame Quest was in bed, but considerably better. Her heart was stronger and she was more at peace now that Michael was with her. He sat close to her, holding one of her frail hands. Her eyes were half melancholy, half glad when they rested upon his strong, brown face.

'It is difficult for me to associate my

boy with a gypsy outlaw,' she said quietly. 'But I do not mind what you have done, or what you are. I am only thankful to God that I can have the chance, before I die, to make reparation for my many injustices to you in the past.'

'Do not think about it, Mother,' Michael smiled. 'I have forgotten.'

'We wronged you greatly. But now you will come into your own.'

'Rina and I cannot stay, Mother,' Michael said gently. 'The Castle and all that is in it is for you.'

Madame Quest argued and protested. She was only too willing to accept Rina as her daughter-in-law, to do everything to make her happy. She implored him not to leave her alone.

'You must stay, Michael. You and Rina are all I have now.'

Michael's brow clouded.

'I have promised my people to return to them. I cannot break my word.

'Your place is here. You are Michael

Quest,' she reminded him, 'the High-Excellency of the Castle.'

'It is impossible for me to stay. I cannot desert the tribe. Rina and I wish to return to them. You must try to understand and forgive me.'

Madame Quest sighed deeply. She saw that it was useless to argue further.

'Lionel and I drove you from us,' she said sadly. 'I have no right now to make demands upon you.'

Michael kissed her hand.

'We will often see you, Mother.'

'And if you have a son, isn't his place here?'

Michael's pulses thrilled. If he should have a son! Rina's son! That would be the ultimate.

'When that happens, Mother, my wife and child shall come to you for awhile. But our lives are dedicated to the tribe. We have chosen that way.'

'You were always a determined boy,' Madame Quest smiled. 'Well, I must accept your decision. Now you leave me, my dear, and tell Rina what you mean to do.'

Michael left the bedroom and walked on to the terrace. Rina met him, her great eyes shining.

'Darling,' he said. 'I have told Mother. She understands.'

'I am glad, Michael,' Rina nodded. 'I have no wish to stay in the Castle. No wish at all. You can never be Michael Quest to me. Only Miska, my gypsy lover.'

'My sweet, my darlingest,' he said, taking her in his arms. 'I also want to go back to the mountains. We will leave after the funeral.'

Michael carried out his word. Two days later, he and Rina left the solemn pageantry of the Castle behind them, and rode back to the mountains to their simple cave, and to the wild lawless tribe who had known that Miska would go back to them and that he would keep his promise.

There was rejoicing and feasting at the return of Miska and Rina of the

Red-Hair, his wife. But when the stars dazzled the sky, and the moon shone across the trees, the young couple crept away and rode hand in hand into the forest which they loved, and where they had first been lovers.

There, Michael Quest was forgotten. It was Miska who built for his wife a bed of sweet-smelling moss and dried leaves, canopied with green boughs. It was Miska who sang to her, thrillingly, as he had sung on the drifting barge on the Danube.

That night, in each other's arms, they found heaven again. Rina of the Red-Hair slept in the strong, warm arms of Miska, her gypsy lover.

10

One warm sunlit morning, not quite a year later, a mysterious silence hung over the gypsy encampment in the mountains. A brooding silence such as one experiences in the early hours of the morning, just before the dawn breaks. But the sun was high in the heavens and the gypsies had long since been up, drunk their coffee and eaten their breakfast round their campfires.

All was very quiet. Every man and woman of the tribe sat still, the men smoking, the women sewing and trying to still the sudden wail of a baby, or laughter of a restless child. Every now and again somebody whispered:

'When will it be?'

Or:

'It is time now, surely . . . at any moment we shall hear the guns.'

There was a tense atmosphere of

265

excitement, subdued but strong. Hundreds of pairs of eyes were turned in the direction of Foracza, eager and expectant. Hundreds of gypsy hearts beat fast with a hope that they shared with the beloved leader of their tribe.

A month ago Miska and his wife had left their mountain home. Rina of the Red-Hair had been taken down to the Castle. For although she had wanted to remain here — wanted her child to be born amongst the gypsies — it had been Michael, himself, who insisted upon taking her to the Castle.

Rina was not as strong as the women of the tribe. She was brave — who knew that better than himself? But this was the one time when he would not let her take a risk. He had dedicated his life to his people, but for a few weeks they could do without him, knowing that he would come back.

Old Madame Quest still lived. And although still frail, the life had by no means gone out of her yet. She clung to it with a tenacity which astonished even her physician. She had so much to live for now. She would not die, she said, until she had looked upon the face of her son's child.

Of course it must be a son. Not a soul in Foracza but wished the baby to be a boy. For that would mean there was yet another heir for the Quests.

For weeks now, peasants and gypsies had come pouring into the Castle grounds, leaving their humble offerings for the unborn child. There was a room full of the pathetic presents, all of which Rina accepted with gratitude and found most touching tributes to hers and to Michael's popularity. Little embroidered Hungarian garments . . . hand-knitted shawls . . . fine lace . . . toys carved from local wood by master craftsmen . . . cakes and sweetmeats made by the women of Foracza . . . gypsy trinkets brought by the tribe, who came on foot to hand their treasures in at the Castle.

And now Rina's hour had come. And while the tribe waited for the news which meant as much to them as to the rest of Foracza, the Castle was in a most unusual state of excitement. A specialist had arrived from Budapest to attend to Rina as well as the Castle physician. He was with Rina now. And downstairs in the great hall, Michael waited with his mother, pacing up and down, smoking cigarette after cigarette, heart hammering, an unspoken prayer on his lips.

The old lady sat placidly knitting, pausing now and again to comfort him.

'Foolish boy . . . there is no need to behave like a caged tiger. Rina will be all right. Is it not a natural event? Why, you are worse than your father, when you and poor Lionel were born.'

'If anything should happen to her . . . if she should die!' Michael said, his forehead wet, his eyes frantic. 'I should never forgive myself, *never*!'

'Tch! Tch!' chuckled the old lady, 'this is not the time to speak of death but of birth, my dear. Rina is a normal, healthy girl — indeed she has led such an existence in the mountains lately, that she should be far better fitted to bear a child than if she had lived a soft life in London.'

'I hope to God you're right,' said Michael.

He walked out of the Castle and into the gardens. Trees and flower-beds were bathed in mellow sunlight. It was a heavenly morning, thought Michael, and a fitting one for the birth of Rina's child. His lovely, beloved young wife! How unutterably happy they had been together this last year. If that happiness should end now, it would be an appalling tragedy.

With anxious eyes, he looked up at the windows of her room. In there, she was with her nurses and the doctors. She was *suffering* . . . *that* was an unbearable thought to him. Yet when he had seen her a few hours ago, she had laughed at him and sent him away, telling him not to fret. All was going well and she was enormously proud and pleased because she was so soon to bring their child into the world.

He had left her room in a daze . . . hardly seeing the lovely little clothes which had been laid out by the nurses . . . each garment embroidered with a silken crest . . . and the cradle carved from mountain oak, and with a canopy of palest blue silk . . . that same cradle in which he and his brother Lionel had lain so many years ago. It was waiting for his child . . . *her* child. Michael could not see or think clearly. He had only known then, as he knew now, that he loved Rina better than life and that she would always come first with him. First and foremost before any son or daughter whom she might bear to him.

He turned from her window to the mountains which were veiled by a golden haze of heat. He thought:

'My people are up there. Soon we shall be back with them . . . And we shall be glad.'

He had missed his gypsy life during the weeks which he had been down at the Castle with Rina, and he knew that she, too, had missed it. Neither of them cared for the luxurious and artificial existence which they had to lead with his mother.

Suddenly he swung round to the Castle again. He heard someone call his name.

It was his mother, standing in the doorway beckoning him with her stick.

The sweat broke out on his forehead. He ran madly across the lawn and reached the side of his mother, panting.

'Well, what is it?'

The old lady's eyes were wet and her voice trembled as she answered him:

'Michael, my darling, great news . . . great news . . . I am overcome . . .'

'What is it?' he repeated hoarsely.

Madame Quest answered:

'A boy, Michael. Rina has given you a son.'

He did not answer. His heart was too full for words, but he thought:

'She has given me not only a son but the *world*!'

He bent, kissed his mother's cheek,

then rushed up the stairs two at a time, to see the mother of his son.

Up in the mountains, the gypsies had been roused from their brooding silence by the sound of a gun. One reverberation, then two. It was to be two for a boy, Miska had told them. Every man, woman and child leapt to their feet, and from a thousand throats there came a roar of acclamation:

'*A son!* The son of Miska, our leader, has been born!'

There was a wild rush for wine, then; for toasting and feasting and dancing, to celebrate an event which was as important to them as to the Quests. For it was not only a son of Michael Quest's who had entered the world this day, but the son of Miska the Gypsy.

In the beautiful room wherein all the heirs of the Quests had made their first appearance, Rina lay on her pillows with her child in her arms, one hand locked fast in Michael's.

'Look at him, darling,' she kept saying to him. '*Look* at him.'

But his gaze was upon her, adoring that lovely face which was pale and weary after her ordeal. Yet she seemed to him even more beautiful. The crown of motherhood sat gloriously upon Rina.

He said:

'How wonderful you are.'

'Yes, but so is your son. Just *look*, Michael.'

He dragged his gaze from her to the tiny flower-like face in the crook of her arm. Manlike, he saw little beauty in those pink crumpled features. But he noticed suddenly the silky down on the tiny head, and it brought an exclamation from him:

'Rina, my darling, he has *red hair* like yours.'

'Yes, that's rather a blow, isn't it? I wanted him to have black hair like yours.'

Michael put out a finger and touched the soft scarlet silk on his son's head.

'No, I'm glad he is like his mother. We've never had a 'red' Quest. You have

273

started a new line, Rina.'

'And what about a red-haired gypsy?' she laughed.

'Yes, he'll be that if he leads a double life like his father.'

'Will he?'

'If he's at all like his father, he will never keep away from the mountains,' said Michael.

At that moment, Michael-the-Second opened his eyes. Mother and father looked at him eagerly, and in awe, as though a miracle had been performed. Then Rina said in a hushed voice:

'His eyes are *your* colour, darling. And of *course* he will be like you in every way. Strong and handsome — and marvellous.'

Michael bent and kissed her and then his son.

'I've been told I mustn't stay. You've got to sleep. And soon, my darling, we shall go back to the mountains — the three of us. And we shall show our people the little red-haired gypsy whom you have given us.'